He glanced over his shoulder to see if Shani had reappeared yet. She was just passing the ledge where they'd all sat for their picnic. 'Hurry up, slow coach,' he called to her.

At that same moment he saw an animal leap out from behind a rock higher up the slope. Without breaking its stride, it ran down the hill towards Shani.

For a split second, Jake thought it was another wolf, but then he realized that it couldn't be. It was dark and scrawny and much bigger than a wolf. Snarling savagely, it hurtled closer and closer to Shani, who hadn't seen it yet.

Pure terror flooded Jake, almost paralysing him. 'Look out!' he managed to shout, the words coming out in a strangled squeak.

Also in the Safari Summer *series*

Pride
Hunted
Tusk
Chase
Instinct

Other series by Lucy Daniels,
published by Hodder Children's Books

Animal Ark

Animal Ark Pets

Little Animal Ark

Animal Ark Hauntings

Dolphin Diaries

LUCY DANIELS

SAFARI SUMER

HOWL

*Hodder
Children's
Books*

a division of Hodder Headline Limited

To Dr Claudio Sillero,
tireless friend of the Ethiopian Wolves

Special thanks to Andrea Abbott

Thanks also to everyone at the Born Free Foundation
(www.bornfree.org.uk) for reviewing the
wildlife information in this book

Text copyright © 2004 Working Partners Limited
Created by Working Partners Limited, London W6 0QT
Illustrations copyright © 2004 Pulsar Studios (Beehive Illustration)

First published in Great Britain in 2004 by Hodder Children's Books

For more information about Lucy Daniels,
please visit www.animalark.co.uk

10 9 8 7 6 5 4 3 2 1

A Catalogue record for this book is available from the British Library.

ISBN 0 340 87852 5

Typeset in Palatino by Avon DataSet Ltd,
Bidford-on-Avon, Warwickshire

Printed and bound in Great Britain by Clays Ltd, St Ives plc

The paper and board used in this paperback by Hodder Children's
Books are natural recyclable products made from wood grown in
sustainable forests. The manufacturing processes conform to the
environmental regulations of the country of origin.

Hodder Children's Books
a division of Hodder Headline Limited
338 Euston Road
London NW1 3BH

ONE

The eighteen seater plane raced down the runway of Addis Ababa airport, the twin engines screaming as they built up speed. Inside the cabin, thirteen-year-old Jake Berman looked excitedly out of his window. *Not long now and we'll be in Lalibela*, he thought.

The big jets that were parked outside the whitewashed terminal building flashed past as if they were moving too. A huge giraffe logo on the tail of one of the Air Tanzania Boeings went by in a blur and Jake pointed it out to his best friend, twelve-year-old Shani Rafiki, who was sitting next to him.

'That's probably the plane we've just got off.'

'Probably,' Shani agreed.

They had left Musabi, the game reserve in Tanzania where Jake lived with his mum and step-dad, Rick, before dawn. At Dar es Salaam they had boarded the plane for Ethiopia. Now they were on the last leg of their journey, the short flight north to the town of Lalibela where Jake and Shani were going to meet members of a conservation team fighting to save one of the most threatened animals on earth, the Ethiopian Wolf.

Jake stared through the perspex window. The plane banked over Addis Ababa, low enough for him to see cars and buses jostling for space on the roads, and people hurrying along crowded pavements, but high enough for everything to look like miniatures. Soon they'd left Addis behind and were flying above green and brown patchwork fields, more densely populated than the endless golden savannah of Tanzania.

Since coming to live on the game reserve a year ago, Jake had had some fantastic adventures, and animals like elephants, cheetahs, lions and the highly endangered black rhino now seemed as familiar as English foxes and squirrels. But this would be the first time Jake had a chance to meet Africa's only wolf.

'I still can't believe our luck,' he remarked to Shani. Below them, the shadow of the aeroplane moved swiftly like a giant bird across the steep hills and craggy slopes that marked the beginning of the highlands where the wolves lived.

'It wasn't just luck,' Shani retorted. 'Don't forget how hard we worked to win that award.'

She was referring to the East African Young Conservationist Award. Jake and Shani had been selected as this year's winners for a project they'd done on man's involvement in the wild.

'Yes, but it was thanks to the rhinos that we ended up doing the project,' Jake reminded her. 'If we hadn't come across that black rhino that was snared and shot just for his horn, we wouldn't have had the idea.' Worst of all, the man behind the poaching operation had been staying in one of the guest chalets at Musabi, pretending to be an honest businessman. 'I mean, something good had to come out of the misery he caused,' Jake finished sombrely.

Shani nodded. 'That rhino didn't die for nothing. In a way, we can thank him that *Safari World* never happened.'

Safari World was the name of a sprawling chain of hotels that two genuine businessmen had planned to build in Tanzania and some of the neighbouring countries. But after Musabi had worked its magic on the visitors, and when they discovered that their colleague, Mr Samsudin, had been responsible for the death of a rhino, they changed their plans completely. *Safari World* would never see the light of day. Instead, there would only be a small ecologically friendly lodge near Musabi called Rhino Retreat, for guests who wanted to see black rhinos – and all the other incredible African wildlife – in their natural habitat.

It was this change of heart that had inspired Jake and Shani to do their project. Over several weekends when they were home from their Dar es Salaam boarding school, they had interviewed the people involved in the new development, and taken photographs and even made some video footage of the emerging lodge.

It had been a lot of work, but their efforts had paid off. Despite stiff competition from students all over Tanzania, and from as far afield as Kenya and Uganda, Jake and Shani had been presented with the award at a ceremony held a few weeks ago in their school hall.

For Jake, it was a huge honour to be selected as joint young conservationist of the year, but what was even more brilliant was the prize: a trip to the Wollo region of Ethiopia to help out on the Ethiopian Wolf Conservation Programme. Lalibela, where he and Shani were headed, was the nearest town to the Wollo district; this was where the conservation team was based, headed by two Ethiopians – a biologist named Gabriel Bellezza, and his wife, Gite, who was the programme's chief vet.

Jake was roused from his thoughts when the pilot called out to his passengers from the cockpit, his voice half-drowned by the droning of the engines. 'Hilltop monastery coming up on the left. We'll go in for a closer look.'

Jake's stomach lurched as the plane dived towards a flat-topped mountain then flew level with the ancient but still intact stone monastery that stood alone on the rocky plateau, its brown walls contrasting with the clear blue sky around it. Jake glimpsed a few men dressed in bright purple robes coming out from a doorway and he guessed they must be priests or monks. But before he could get a closer look at them, the plane climbed steeply again and Jake lost sight of the men and the building where they worshipped.

'It's like being on a joyride,' he laughed to Shani as the plane levelled out. He'd heard how the pilots of the smaller aircraft in Ethiopia often swooped down close to interesting sights to give their passengers a good view.

'Yeah. It's much more fun than the flight from Dar,' agreed Shani.

A suntanned young man sitting behind Jake and Shani leaned forward with his arms resting on the back of Jake's seat. 'Are you two going mule trekking in the mountains?' His accent was Australian.

'Not this time,' Jake answered, twisting round. 'We're going to help out with the Ethiopian Wolf Conservation Programme.' Mule trekking sounded really cool, and it was definitely something he'd like to do one day, but being involved with the wolves was much closer to his heart.

'Ethiopian Wolf?' echoed the Australian. 'I read something about those animals when I was planning this trip. They're also called Simien Foxes, or red jackals, aren't they?'

'That's right. But for something that has so many names, there's precious few of them left,' Jake said.

The statistics were depressing. The wolves were classed as critically endangered and there were probably only about five hundred of them left in the Ethiopian highlands.

'Sounds pretty grim,' said the Australian sympathetically. 'Let's hope the conservation team can make a difference. How did you two get involved?'

Shani told him about the award and the project they'd done.

The young man looked impressed. 'It sounds like you know what you're talking about. Does that mean you've done this kind of thing before? Save animals, I mean?'

'Sort of,' Jake said modestly, thinking about chimps and the pair of lion cubs, among others, he'd helped to rescue. And then there was Bina, the tiny baby dik-dik he and Rick had taken home to hand-rear after her mother was snatched by an eagle.

The plane turned sharply to the right and began its final descent. Jack felt excitement fizzing inside him; the flight had been fun, but now he couldn't wait to get off the plane and meet his first wolf. Out of the window he saw a dusty-looking settlement on the top of a flat mountain. It looked more of a sprawling village than a town, with squat flat-roofed buildings set amidst a surprising number of leafy trees. From the air, there seemed to be hardly any motorized traffic and the roads were little more than narrow tracks running between the buildings.

'Are you just here for the mule trekking?' Shani asked the Australian.

He grinned. 'That, and this country's incredible history. Did you know they carved churches out of the rocks round here, nearly a thousand years ago?'

Shani shook her head, and he passed her a well-thumbed guidebook from his rucksack. 'Here, have a look,' he offered, holding it open at the history section.

Shani looked at the pictures of the incredible mountain churches, then flicked through the pages until she came to a piece about the country's wildlife. 'And this is why we're here,' she declared, turning to a picture of an animal that looked a bit like a jackal. The caption read: *Ethiopian Wolf* (*Canis Simensis*).

Jake looked appreciatively at the beautiful creature in the photograph. Its coat was mainly red, like a fox, but its throat, underparts and the inside of its legs were white. It had broad pointed ears and a thick brush-like tail that was black on top and white underneath. Looking over its shoulder and staring straight at the camera, the wolf had a gentle, trusting expression on its face. It could almost have been someone's pet dog. Except for one big difference.

Domestic dogs were probably the most abundant canine species in the world. The Ethiopian Wolf was the rarest.

TWO

'Jake and Shani?'

Hearing their names above the hubbub in the small airport building that rather resembled a village hall, Jake looked round.

A couple in their mid-twenties were coming toward him and Shani. They were both tall, with dark hair and bronzed complexions. The woman wore her hair in neat braids under a brightly coloured scarf, and she was dressed in a long floral skirt and a plain red top.

'Hello, I'm Gabriel,' said the man when he reached Jake and Shani, 'and this is my wife, Gite.'

Gite smiled at the two friends. 'You *are* Jake and Shani, aren't you?'

'That's us,' Jake answered.

'Welcome to Lalibela and congratulations on your big win,' said Gite warmly. 'We thought you really deserved it. Your project was outstanding.'

'You've read it?' asked Shani, surprised.

'Yes. The award committee sent us a copy last

8

week,' said Gabriel. 'We were very impressed with the way you showed how man could be in harmony with his natural surroundings. Too many projects on that sort of theme only look at the negative impact humans have on the world.'

Jake felt a rush of pride.

'Of course, that's exactly what we're trying to achieve with our programme – encourage people to co-operate so that the world doesn't lose another species,' put in Gite.

'And standing around here isn't going to help much,' smiled Gabriel. He took Shani's rucksack and swung it over one shoulder. 'Let's go. There's a lot of work to be done.'

'What kind of work?' Jake asked eagerly.

'Well, there's a lot of routine stuff, like taking DNA samples from droppings and collecting data about the different packs,' said Gabriel.

'Then there are the vaccination clinics to inoculate domestic dogs against diseases that could spread to the wolf population,' Gite added.

'Like rabies?' said Shani.

'That, and others like distemper.'

'Of course there are exciting parts to our work too,' said Gabriel, pushing open the door to let Gite and Shani go through. 'We monitor the packs continually to keep an eye on their health and their numbers, and to make sure they're not being persecuted.'

'That means you go out tracking them?' Jake asked

hopefully, following Gabriel outside on to a dusty pavement.

'Not as you would a rhino or pride of lions. You see, we know the packs very well and where their home ranges are, so we ride to those areas . . .' The rest of his sentence was drowned out by a car speeding past, so close that Jake could have touched it. Gabriel automatically put a protective arm in front of Gite and Shani. 'Maniac,' he muttered under his breath.

Jake picked up the conversation again. 'You were saying you ride to the wolves' territories.' He pictured the conservation team going out on motorbikes or in a jeep.

'Yes, on mules,' Gite said.

Jake stopped dead in the middle of the road. 'Hey, that means we get to go mule trekking too!' he exclaimed. 'Brilliant.'

A crowded mini-bus taxi suddenly appeared as if from nowhere and blared its horn at Jake. He jumped out of its way and in two strides reached the others on the opposite pavement.

'You need to watch out for those in the towns,' Gite advised Jake.

'Yes, I know. We've got taxis like that in Tanzania too,' he said, feeling rather embarrassed. 'I think I'd rather ride a mule than risk my life in one of those.'

Gabriel winked at Shani then said to Jake, 'You might think differently about that after you've been in the saddle for eight hours.'

'I bet I won't,' Jake argued. 'Especially if it means we'll get close to the wolves.'

'I'm afraid the first day's trek won't take us to the wolves,' Gite said apologetically as they walked towards a row of cars parked in the shade of some towering eucalyptus trees. 'We have to get to Abuna Joseph first.'

Shani frowned. 'Where's that?'

'It's a holy mountain in a remote part of the highlands, where several packs of wolves live. We have a camp up there so that we can be close to the packs,' Gabriel explained.

'When do we go up to the camp?' Jake asked.

'We start first thing in the morning,' said Gabriel. 'It's the height of the breeding season so we're doing regular checks to see if any pups have been born.'

'Brilliant,' Jake said. He hadn't bargained on seeing pups. Things just kept getting better. Still, he was a little disappointed they couldn't start then and there. He'd banked on seeing wolves that same day. But it was already half way through the afternoon and he realized that with the camp an eight hour trek away, they'd never reach it before dark.

Gite stopped next to a small truck. 'This is ours.' She unlocked the driver's door then gestured to Shani to get in the other side. Jake and Gabriel were to ride on the open back.

Jake slung his rucksack over the side and was about to climb in when he saw the Australian tourist waiting to board a dilapidated-looking bus a little further along.

Jake waved. 'Have a great holiday,' he called.

'Thanks, mate. And make sure you save those wolves,' came the reply.

'Friend of yours?' Gabriel asked Jake.

'Not really. We met him on the plane. He's going to look at the rock churches, then he's going mule trekking,' Jake explained, climbing into the truck.

'That means he's probably going to Debark next,' said Gabriel. He held Shani's door for her so that she could climb into the cab.

Shani shook her head. 'No, he's only just arrived. He's getting *on* the bus, not *dis*embarking,' she politely corrected him.

Gabriel broke out laughing so that Shani looked completely confused.

Jake was equally puzzled until Gite explained. 'Debark is a town where the mule treks start. It's at the foot of the Simien Mountains to the west.'

Shani looked very embarrassed but Gabriel quickly put her out of her misery. 'Don't worry, Shani. I love a play on words, even accidental ones. And anyway, English is not my first language. I speak Amharic and Italian a lot better so I could easily have made a mistake.' He waited for Shani to climb into the cab, then shut her door and swung himself over the tailgate of the truck.

Jake soon realized that the town was much bigger

than it had seemed from the air. There was a lot more traffic here than there had been at the airport and Gite had to drive slowly through narrow streets that were jammed with trucks and taxis and people buying goods from colourful kerb-side stalls.

From the open back of the truck, Jake caught the exotic whiff of spicy aromas. 'Smells delicious,' he remarked to Gabriel, who nodded and said, 'It's injera. Made from a cereal called tej. You'll get to taste it yourself very soon.'

'Great.' Jake hoped that it was as tasty as it smelled. He wasn't exactly adventurous when it came to food, and since coming to Africa he'd had a few nasty surprises when people had dished up curry which was so hot it had just about burnt the roof of his mouth off.

They drove on through the crowded streets where goats, sheep and cows wandered around, unruffled by all the human commotion. Others stood in the shade of mud-walled buildings for even though Lalibela was in the highlands, the sun beat down strongly from a clear blue sky. A couple of goats scampered across the road some way in front of the truck. They were followed by a small boy and three skinny dogs who herded the goats into a narrow alleyway.

They passed a sports stadium which reminded Jake that Ethiopian athletes were among the fastest in the world; he'd seen some of their incredible long-distance runners and sprinters when watching television coverage of the Olympics.

Not far from the stadium, a sign pointed to a hospital and Jake caught sight of a small concrete building half-hidden by eucalyptus trees. They were on the outskirts of the town now and the mountains rose up a short distance away. *That's where the wolves are*, Jake thought with a shiver of pleasure.

The conservation team's compound was a few blocks away from the hospital. As the truck drew up in front of the bamboo fence surrounding the property, a uniformed man opened the gate.

'Thank you,' called Gabriel. 'That's Faisal, our sabanjia,' he explained.

'Sabanjia?' Jake echoed.

'Watchman. Just making sure we're not troubled by thieves.'

'Crumbs!' said Jake, climbing over the side of the truck. 'Do you get lots of burglaries here?'

'Not really,' Gabriel reassured him. 'But like anywhere, there are criminals. We have our fair share of bandits in this area.'

'Is that why visitors have to have minders?' Jake asked. The Ethiopian consul in Tanzania had told Jake and Shani that they could expect to be accompanied everywhere in Ethiopia by an official.

'Yes, that's right,' said Gabriel.

Shani had overheard the conversation as she was

getting out of the cab. 'I suppose sabanjias are like the askaris we have in Tanzania.'

'Pretty much,' Gabriel agreed.

Jake heaved his rucksack out the back of the truck and glanced around. In the centre of the yard was a small house with mud walls and a corrugated iron roof. There were three other smaller buildings in the yard, little more than single rooms which were also made from mud and iron.

'Coffee everyone?' Gite offered, going toward the main house.

'Er, thanks,' replied Jake.

Shani stared at him in surprise. She knew Jake hated coffee! But he didn't want to seem rude by saying no, and it wouldn't kill him to have one cup. He gave Shani a meaningful look, to warn her not to let on that he was just being polite.

'As you see, we don't have a lot of room,' said Gabriel as they went inside the simply furnished house. 'I hope you don't mind sleeping rough.' He pointed to a couple of mattresses on the woven bamboo floor.

There were two doors leading off the room while in one corner there was a phone and a computer on a desk and next to it, a set of shelves lined with books and files.

'Sleeping rough's no problem for me,' Shani said cheerfully. 'I usually end up on the floor when our relatives come to visit us.'

'And we've brought our sleeping bags,' Jake added.

'You'll definitely need those up at the mountain camp,' said Gite. 'It's freezing there at night. Now, have a seat while I make the coffee.' She went over to a small coal stove. On a shelf next to it was a bag of coffee beans, a jug-like pot and a hand grinder.

Jake and Shani sat down on low stools and watched Gite grinding the beans then pouring them into the spout of the jug. Next she put the jug on the stove and before long, the room was filled with the aroma of fresh coffee.

'Smells good,' said Shani, winking at Jake.

Jake pulled a face. To him it smelt like mud being boiled, but he kept his opinion to himself. He looked around the walls of the room, half-expecting to see photographs of wolves, but there were none. The only picture was of a whale and that was on a year planner pinned up on the wall behind the desk.

'You're wondering where the wolves are, aren't you?' Gabriel guessed.

'Yeah. It's kind of weird to come all this way to see wolves and end up looking at a whale,' Jake grinned.

'I can fix that.' Gabriel went to the bookshelf and took down a cardboard folder. 'This will give you some idea of what we do.' He pulled up a stool between Jake and Shani, then sat down and opened the file.

On the first page were the words ABUNA JOSEPH PROJECT.

Jake expected the rest of the file to be a scientific report of the conservation programme but it turned out to be more like a photograph album filled with pictures of wolves.

'These are the animals we've been working to save,' said Gabriel, slowly turning the pages.

There were shots of wolves in small packs, of females with litters of cubs, and of single wolves hunting. Some pictures showed Gabriel and Gite and other members of the conservation team out on their mules, or in villages where they were vaccinating domestic dogs. Another picture showed a few huts on the side of the mountain with Gite standing in a doorway.

'That's the camp at Abuna Joseph,' Gabriel explained. He came to the last photograph, a close-up of a large, handsome wolf standing on a rocky plateau amid stubby heather-like plants.

Even though Jake had yet to see a wolf for real, he could tell that this was a particularly magnificent one. The russet-coated animal stood tall and straight-backed, staring into the camera lens with an air of confidence – like a lord surveying his land, Jake thought.

'That's Tullu,' said Gabriel. 'A legendary alpha male. All the others seemed to treat him as if he was a chief. He's the father of quite a few of the wolves in Abuna Joseph.'

'He's divine!' breathed Shani.

'Yes, he was,' said Gabriel. 'Quite superb.'

'Was?' Jake frowned and looked up at Gabriel.

A shadow passed across his dark, handsome face. 'Yes, we lost him to rabies. He and sixteen others, a few years ago.'

'Seventeen wolves died of rabies?' Jake gasped. And to think there were less than five hundred Ethiopian Wolves left in the whole world! He did a quick mental calculation. Seventeen out of five hundred: that was something like three per cent of the population being wiped out in one go.

Gita had come across and was leaning over Gabriel's shoulder to look at Tullu. 'We traced the outbreak to a dog that belonged to a shepherd who'd been grazing his sheep near Abuna Joseph.' She sighed. 'That'll give you an idea of what we're up against,' she said, a note of hopelessness in her voice. 'We worked day and night for months to contain that outbreak. We must have covered hundreds of square kilometres combing the mountains for rabid dogs.'

'And we never know when the disease will hit us again,' said Gabriel. 'That's why we have to keep encouraging people to vaccinate their dogs.'

Somewhere outside, a dog barked, a high-pitched, warning yelp that sent a shiver down Jake's spine. There were so many dogs in this country, and any one of them could be carrying the disease that would send the Ethiopian Wolf into the history books forever.

THREE

'Please stand still,' Jake begged his mule. For a third time he tried to heave the saddle on to the animal's back. The dark-brown animal blinked at Jake then skipped a few steps to one side so that Jake ended up hoisting the saddle into thin air.

'Need any help?' chuckled Shani. She was already sitting on her mule, a light-grey one which had given her no trouble at all. It had snuffled into her neck when she tied her rolled-up sleeping bag to the back of the saddle, and stood still while she saddled it.

It was shortly after breakfast the next morning and Jake and Shani had come outside to choose their mules from a pen in the yard, ready for the trek up to Abuna Joseph. Gite and Gabriel were still busy inside, doing some last-minute paperwork and making phone calls before their departure.

'I'm fine,' Jake insisted while under his breath he muttered, 'but it looks like I chose the wrong mule.'

Shani tried to look solemn but her twinkling eyes gave her away. 'I don't think you're going to have

19

much luck,' she commented as the mule suddenly kicked its back legs, then skittered over to the other side of the yard where it stopped to munch the tufts of grass growing next to the bamboo fence.

Jake gritted his teeth. He'd been in all sorts of tricky situations with animals before, ranging from being chased up a tree by a lion, to nearly being flattened by an elephant. No mule was going to get the better of him. 'Now look here, mule,' he said, going over to it. 'You and I have a long way to go so we might as well be friends.'

The mule raised his head and, for a second, Jake thought the animal was grinning at him when it curled back his top lip to reveal a row of yellowing teeth. But this was no friendly smile. Instead the mule opened his mouth and began to bray at the top of his voice as if he was being saddled with barbed wire.

'Now what?' Jake said, looking round helplessly and going bright red when he saw Gite and Gabriel coming outside. They were followed by a man called Mengistu who'd arrived half an hour earlier on a big black horse. Mengistu had been sent by the Ministry of Agriculture to be Jake and Shani's minder.

Faisal the sabanjia appeared from one of the outbuildings.

'Oh dear,' laughed Gite. 'Emperor's having one of his bad days.' She must have seen Jake's embarrassment because she quickly added, 'It's not your fault, Jake. Emperor is just very temperamental. He'll settle down soon enough.'

Grinning broadly, Faisal came over and held the mule so that Jake finally managed to get the saddle on. Then he quickly swung himself on to it before Emperor could decide to get up to any more of his tricks.

Gite and Gabriel fetched their mules too and Mengistu untied his horse, then they all trailed out of the yard, Faisal closing the gate behind them.

With Gabriel in the lead and Mengistu at the back, they trotted down the street, passing white-robed pilgrims going to church. Jake was pleasantly surprised at how willingly Emperor set off; he'd half-expected the mule to refuse to leave the compound.

'So far, so good,' he said quietly.

Before long, the riders joined a rutted track that led upwards into the foothills. The path quickly grew steeper and more rocky so that Jake began to appreciate just how strong and sure-footed the mules were. Higher and higher they climbed until, an hour or so later, Lalibela was hardly visible. Just the tin roofs catching the sun and a small aeroplane coming in to land showed that there was a town far below.

'It feels like we're on top of the world,' Shani remarked.

'Now you can see why Ethiopia is called the Roof of Africa,' said Gite.

Eventually, the track joined another that ran the

length of a long ridge. To the north, towering rocky peaks touched the sky, and in the south, there was a grassy plateau. Jake thought it seemed a very remote, unforgiving place and yet there were a lot of people around, some of them riding horses or mules, others herding sheep and cattle, or walking behind teams of short-legged oxen to plough the steeply sloping fields.

Often, young children would run alongside the mules calling out to Jake and Shani, 'Do you have a pen for me? Do you have a birr?'

'What's a birr?' Shani called over her shoulder to Gite, who was riding in front of Mengistu.

'Money,'

'Sorry, no birr,' said Shani to a little boy jogging next to her with his arm outstretched. 'But there's a pen in my backpack. When we come down this way I'll give it to you if I see you again.'

'How many wolves are up there?' Jake asked Gite, half-turning in his saddle to look back at her.

'We think about forty-five adults altogether in Wollo,' she replied. 'About twenty of those live in four family groups in Abuna Joseph.'

'That's only just a little more than the number that died from rabies,' Jake commented. The epidemic a few years ago must have halved the population in the area. It would only take one more outbreak to clear Abuna Joseph of wolves completely.

After a few hours, Gabriel stopped his mule next to a mountain stream. 'Time for a rest,' he announced.

'How far have we come?' Shani asked, sliding off her mule.

'About twenty-five kilometres,' Gabriel told her. 'But it's not only distance we've travelled, we've also come very high up.'

'What's the altitude here?' said Jake.

'Approaching three thousand metres,' said Mengistu, dismounting and lifting the reins over his horse's head. He pointed to the surrounding mountains. 'Some of those peaks are around four thousand metres above sea level.'

'Sheesh!' Jake was pretty sure that, apart from when he'd flown in aeroplanes, he'd never been this high up before. Once, before he came to Africa, he'd hiked up Mount Snowdon in Wales with his class, but that was only just over a thousand metres high.

While the mules and Mengistu's horse drank from the stream, their riders sat on the stony ground and ate injera, a kind of pancake left over from supper the night before. Jake had been relieved to find that it was quite tasty after all.

But they'd only just started eating when hosts of small children appeared as if from nowhere and surrounded them.

'Hello. What's your name? What's your address? Have you got a birr? Have you got a pen?' they rattled off, all talking together.

Jake fished in his backpack but couldn't find

anything to give them. Shani found the pen she'd promised to the boy earlier. 'I probably wouldn't see him again anyway,' she said, giving it to a shy little girl.

'Ishee,' said the child, a broad smile on her pretty face.

'What does that mean?' Shani asked Gabriel.

'It's a bit like your English word, cool,' the biologist told her.

Mengistu stood up and clapped his hands at the children. They scattered, giggling, then stood some distance away, staring at Jake and Shani as if the two friends were visitors from not only another country but from another planet.

'Are we that bizarre?' Jake asked, feeling uncomfortable.

'No. I think they're just fascinated to see you with us,' said Gite. 'They've seen us dozens of times and are wondering who you are.'

When it was time to go on again, they went to fetch their mules from the stream.

'Come on, Emperor,' Jake said, taking the reins.

Shani's mule, whose name was Angel, needed no urging and went straight to Shani as soon as she saw her approaching.

Jake had no such luck. He tried to lead Emperor out of the stream but the animal refused to budge.

Jake rolled his eyes. 'Oh no, not again.' Feeling very irritated, he tugged the reins, but Emperor had anchored himself in the river and was glaring stubbornly at Jake.

'I give up. I'm not fighting with you any more.' Jake dropped the reins and turned away. 'I'd rather walk the rest of the way.' Why was it that he had to end up with such an unco-operative animal when all the others were as good as gold?

Everyone else had mounted and they were watching Jake with a mixture of amusement and sympathy. Jake felt utterly humiliated, especially when Emperor suddenly trotted past and began picking his way up the path without him.

'Hey!' Jake shouted. 'Just hold on a minute, you!' He stormed up the track after Emperor, trying to ignore the stifled chuckles coming from the others.

By the time he caught up with the mule, he was out of breath. 'Are you trying to make a fool of me or what?' he puffed, grabbing the reins. Emperor stopped and Jake pulled himself up into the saddle. 'OK. Let's go now,' Jake said, nudging the mule with his heels.

'Here, let me give you a hand,' said Shani, riding up behind him, and she smacked the mule's rump with the flat of her hand.

Emperor took off as if he was in a race. Jake clung on tightly as the mule scrambled up the track at double speed. Behind him, he could hear the others roaring with laughter. 'It's OK for you,' he called back to them when Emperor finally slowed down, but then he realized how funny he must have looked and he burst out laughing too. 'I think you're just having a lot of fun at my expense,' he said to his mule.

The higher they went, the more rugged the terrain became and Jake was glad to see that here, the steep mountain slopes and deep valleys were often still covered in forests. Man hadn't yet managed to tame the wildest reaches. Still, there were many peasant farmers scratching a living out of small plots of land beside the track. Gite and Gabriel knew several of them and often waved to them in greeting, or stopped for a brief chat.

Once, a farmer hailed them and spoke passionately to Gite and Gabriel in the local language. Jake couldn't understand a word the man said, but the tone of his voice gave away his anger.

'What's he saying?' Shani whispered to Mengistu.

'He says wolves broke through his fence last night and took two of his sheep,' the minder translated.

'Oh no!' said Jake, feeling dismayed.

'The farmer says that if the wolves do it again, he'll have to do what he can to protect his sheep,' Mengistu went on.

'We've heard threats like that before, haven't we, Jake?' said Shani.

Jake knew she was thinking of the herd of elephants that had broken out of a game reserve in Zambia and destroyed the crops on nearby farms. The local community had threatened to kill the elephants if something wasn't done. Luckily for the elephants, Jake's step-dad translocated them to Musabi where there was a lot more food and water which meant the herd didn't have to go in search of new feeding grounds.

'Yep,' Jake agreed grimly. 'The animals might be different, but it's the same situation: wild animals under pressure to find food because their habitat is getting smaller.'

'Except that I don't think we can blame the wolves for this case,' put in Gite.

Shani raised her eyebrows. 'Really? How do you know?'

'We're not in their territory yet,' explained Gite. 'Also wolves aren't nocturnal. They hunt by day, and they go mainly for rodents anyway, like moles and rats. Not sheep.'

'Have you told the farmer that?' asked Shani.

'Many, many times,' sighed Gite. 'But people don't always believe us.'

Gabriel must have come to some sort of agreement with the angry man because they shook hands and the farmer walked away looking a little less anxious.

'What did you say to him?' said Shani.

'That it's probably hyenas or jackals that have been getting through the fence,' said Gabriel. 'Still, we want to generate some goodwill so I've promised to help make his fence predator-proof as soon as I have the time.'

Halfway through the afternoon when the air was growing cooler, the five riders arrived at the mountain camp. This consisted of three modest stone rondavels perched on the western slope of the mountain, their tin roofs glinting in the sunlight. The area was bleak, with little vegetation other than grass and stunted heathery plants, and a few huge and rather odd-looking trees that Jake thought looked like palm trees crossed with sisal plants.

'Funny tree,' he remarked as they rode past one.

'They're giant lobelias,' explained Gabriel. 'Up here plants are either very small or over-sized.'

Jake craned his neck as they neared the camp, trying to get a glimpse of the other team members. Gite had told him there was a field assistant called Bedassa and another vet called Celia. But most of all, he wanted to see a wolf. Up here in the highland wilderness, more than three thousand metres above the sea, there had to be at least one wolf somewhere nearby. But if there was, it was staying well out of sight.

Saddle sore and feeling suddenly rather tired, Jake dismounted from his mule in front of the huts. He staggered as he landed on the ground and realized that he was dizzy and slightly nauseous, and had a thumping headache too. So much for his brag that he'd handle the ride well! He felt so rough that he wondered if he had picked up some kind of tummy bug, or even flu.

Gabriel led his mule towards an enclosure made from bamboo poles and beckoned to Jake and Shani to follow. 'We put the mules in here to keep them safe from hyenas at night,' he explained.

With the mules and Mengistu's horse safely penned in, they went across to the rondavels. 'Coffee time?' said Gabriel, looking hopefully at Gite.

Jake felt his stomach turn. 'Just water for me please, if that's OK,' he said. The cup of coffee he'd had at the compound in Lalibela yesterday was enough to last him a lifetime. It had been black and very strong and he'd had to add masses of sugar before he could even think of swallowing it. And then, on top of that, he'd been wide awake for most of the night. No wonder he wasn't feeling all that good now.

It was cool and dark inside the rondavel. Gite dumped her backpack next to the wall. 'We don't even have mattresses up here, I'm afraid, so choose the spot where you want to sleep.' She turned to Mengistu. 'You might want to share a hut with Bedassa. There'll be more room in there for you.' She pointed outside to one of the other huts.

'Talking of Bedassa,' said Gabriel, 'I wonder where he is? Celia too.'

'Probably still out in the field somewhere,' Gite suggested.

'You're right,' said Gabriel. 'I expect they'll be back soon though. They knew we were arriving today and,' he smiled at Jake and Shani, 'they were looking forward to meeting you. They're keen to hear all about Musabi.'

Ordinarily Jake could have talked for hours about his beloved game reserve, but right now he felt so ill, all he wanted to do was go to sleep. *What's the matter with me?* he wondered crossly. He unrolled his sleeping bag beneath a small window then quickly sat down on as another dizzy spell made him feel as if he was about to faint.

'You OK?' Shani asked.

'Yeah, fine,' Jake said. 'I've just got a bit of a headache.'

Gite frowned. 'You don't look good.' She took a first-aid box out of her backpack. 'I'll give you something for your head.'

'I'm fine,' he insisted. This trip was a once-in-a-lifetime opportunity and he wasn't going to miss a single moment of it.

A shadow fell across the door and when Jake looked up, he saw a man who was tall and dark like Gabriel, and wore a moustache.

'Ah, Bedassa, there you are,' said Gabriel. 'Let me introduce you to our young prize-winners. This is Jake.' He smiled at Jake who was leaning against the wall. 'And Shani.' She was unrolling her sleeping bag but she stopped and said hello to the serious-looking man.

Bedassa nodded to them then said something to

Gabriel in their own language. His tone was urgent and he kept glancing over his shoulder as if he was expecting someone else to arrive. Gite immediately put down the first-aid box and went to stand with the two men.

Jake forgot how ill he felt at once. Something odd was going on. He exchanged a glance with Shani who shrugged to show she was as mystified as he was.

Gabriel must have noticed their bewilderment. 'Sorry. We should use English in front of you. I'll translate. Bedassa thinks one of the wolves might have been bitten.'

Jake felt the blood drain from his face. 'By a rabid dog?'

'We don't know,' said Gite. 'Bedassa didn't see it happen. He just came across the wolf licking a wound on one of its back legs.'

'So how do you know it was a dog bite?' Shani asked reasonably. 'And if it was, that the dog had rabies?'

Gabriel's answer made Jake go cold. 'This morning, Bedassa heard that a couple of dogs belonging to local farmers have died of rabies recently. And yesterday, while he was out patrolling, he saw a scrawny dog disappear down the side of the mountain into a deep gorge. He tried to go after it but the path was too steep.'

'Just because the dog was thin, doesn't mean it had rabies,' Jake pointed out hopefully.

Bedassa looked at Jake. 'No, but it was running all over the place and was foaming at the mouth.'

'And what really worries us,' put in Gabriel, 'is that the dog was coming from the home range of one particular group of wolves, the Ridge. And the wounded wolf belongs to this pack, so if he's been bitten, it means the others are at risk, too.'

FOUR

Jake clenched his fists in frustration. Was this the start of the next devastating rabies epidemic in the area?

'Is there nothing we can do?' he demanded. 'What about vaccinating all the wolves?'

'We would if we could,' said Gite. 'But it's not practical to go out injecting wild animals. The best we can do is what we did last time; step up our patrols and keep an eye open for dogs behaving in a strange way.'

This didn't sound particularly useful. 'What about the wolf that was bitten? Do you just leave him to get rabies?' Jake asked.

'Definitely not,' said Gabriel. 'We'll vaccinate him then put him in quarantine until he has the all clear.'

'Sounds easy, but I bet it isn't,' said Shani. 'It's not like he's a dog that'll just walk in on a lead.'

'No, but he'll ride in on a horse,' said Gite mysteriously. 'And it sounds like he's arriving now.'

Jake opened his mouth to ask what she meant, but shut it when he heard the sound of a horse trotting over the hard ground. Ignoring the weakness in his legs, he followed everyone outside. A fair-haired woman was riding towards the rondavels. Lying across the horse's back just in front of her was the wolf, its body limp as if it was dead.

It was nothing like Jake had imagined his first sighting of a wolf would be. He'd always pictured his first wolf standing proudly on a rock to howl at the moon, or darting across the plateau in pursuit of a rat or mole. Or even just staring inquisitively at him from behind a shrub. Instead, the unfortunate animal was draped unceremoniously over a horse's withers, its eyes glazed and jaw slack, its dangling legs twitching in time with each stride.

'Is it dead?' Shani burst out.

'He's sedated, that's all,' Gite reassured her. She went to meet the horse and rider. 'You did well to catch him so quickly,' she said to the woman, then helped Gabriel and Bedassa to lift the sleeping wolf down from the saddle. Carefully, they lowered the jackal-sized animal to the ground, where Gite was able to examine the wound on his back leg.

To Jake's eyes, it certainly looked like a dog bite. Gite thought so too. 'I can't think what else it could be,' she said.

The rider dismounted and came over to the two friends. She was taller than Jake, and had pale, freckled skin and blue eyes. 'You must be the young conservationists from Tanzania,' she said warmly.

Jake nodded.

'I'm Celia,' continued the woman. 'Gite's assistant.'

Bedassa took the horse's reins from Celia and led the animal towards the enclosure.

'Are you a vet too?' Shani asked Celia.

'That's right,' Celia smiled. 'I trained in London, and this certainly makes a change from treating poodles in Putney, I can tell you!'

'How did you catch the wolf?' Jake asked curiously.

'Bedassa and I set up a trap with a big chunk of fresh meat inside,' Celia explained. 'We were a bit worried others might go in before him, or that we'd end up catching hyenas and jackals instead. Luckily for us, he must have been hungry because he sniffed out the meat in no time at all and went into the cage like a lamb. Once he was inside, I could get close enough to sedate him so that we could get him back here.'

Jake couldn't take his eyes off the wolf. He was surprised to find that it looked much more like a fox than like its closer relative, the grey timber wolf. But this didn't make the rare animal any less magnificent, even when it was sedated. Despite the bite wound, he was in perfect condition, lean and muscular, and his reddish gold coat looked so soft that Jake longed to smooth him. He seldom had a chance to touch the wild animals he came into contact with, mainly because they were hardly ever out for the count like this.

'Would you like to help me carry him to the quarantine pen, Jake?' asked Gabriel.

Jake was at the wolf's side in a flash. He knelt down and stroked the animal's coat, which was as fluffy as he had imagined. Next, he ran his hand up the wolf's long muzzle then lightly traced the outline of one pointed ear. All the time, Jake knew how privileged he was to be touching one of the most threatened animals in the world.

Shani knelt down next to Jake and stroked the wolf's neck and shoulders. 'He feels a lot softer than my dog,' she said quietly.

'Let's get him to the pen before he starts waking up,' said Gabriel. 'I'll support his hindquarters and you can hold his front end, Jake.'

Jake slid his arms under the wolf then, at Gabriel's signal, carefully lifted him up. He was surprised at how light the animal was and realized that Gabriel didn't really need his help. It was just a way of giving Jake an opportunity to handle the animal.

'How much would you say he weighs?' he asked, cradling the wolf's head in the crook of his elbow while his other arm supported its chest and shoulders.

'About eighteen kilograms,' said Gabriel. 'The same as a medium-sized dog.'

'A lot like Bweha I suppose,' said Shani, referring to her own dog again. Gently, she adjusted the wolf's head into a more comfortable position on Jake's arm then walked next to him, keeping a close eye on the sleeping animal.

The quarantine enclosure was a fenced-off area about the size of a tennis court with a bamboo screen running down the side that faced the camp. Gabriel explained that this was to give the wolf some privacy from the humans.

The other three sides of the enclosure looked out to the mountains and Jake could imagine that the wolf would feel quite at home, especially as the inside of the pen was the same as the surrounding area. There was a giant lobelia tree in one corner, and the rocky ground was covered with the usual grass and low shrubs. Only the three-metre-high fence would tell the wolf that he was in captivity.

'Do you often keep wolves here?' Shani asked.

'Only in an emergency,' replied Gite.

Shani darted ahead to open the gate and Jake and Gabriel carried the wolf inside. They placed it on the grassy ground, then everyone clustered round and watched as Gite opened a vet's bag. She put on a pair of latex gloves and cleaned the wound with some disinfectant, passing the used cotton wool to Shani to put in a plastic bag. Next she took out an ampoule and filled a syringe before injecting the medicine into the wolf.

'Is that the vaccine?' said Jake.

'No, it's an antibiotic to prevent other infections,' explained Gite, gesturing to Shani to open the plastic refuse bag wide so she could drop the used syringe into it. She chose another small bottle from the bag. 'This is the vaccine. He gets one now and a booster in three days' time.'

'And then what?' Jake said. 'Do you let him go?'

'Not for a while,' Celia answered while Gite injected the vaccine. 'We'll have to observe him to make sure he doesn't start displaying any rabies symptoms. You see, if this wound *is* a bite from a rabid dog, we can't be sure the vaccine will be effective.'

Jake felt stunned. 'You mean he could still get rabies?'

Celia nodded.

'But rabies vaccines *do* work,' insisted Shani.

'Yes, but only for definite if an animal is vaccinated before it gets bitten,' said Gite. She dropped the second used syringe and the empty ampoule into the plastic bag. 'Still, we have to give this wolf a fighting chance. He's too precious for us to write him off.'

'I know someone who was badly bitten by a dog with rabies,' said Shani, tying a tight knot in the bag. 'He had a whole lot of vaccinations and was fine.'

'Yes, that's how it works in humans,' Gite agreed, 'but it's different in animals. Once the virus is in an animal's system, there is no cure, I'm afraid.' She checked the wolf's wound again before standing up and peeling off her gloves.

'Can't you take blood tests to see if the wolf

develops anti-bodies?' Shani persisted. 'Then you'll be able to tell if he's likely to get rabies.'

'We could, but it's not easy to take blood from a wolf. And even if he has enough anti-bodies, we'd still have to observe him for a few months to make sure he doesn't get rabies. It's what the law says,' explained Celia.

Shani nodded. 'Same as in our country.'

'You seem to know a lot about rabies,' said Gite.

'My mum's a nurse,' Shani told her.

Jake saw one of the wolf's ears twitch, and its eyelids started flickering. 'He's waking up,' he whispered.

The wolf opened his eyes and looked straight at Jake.

'OK, everyone,' said Gabriel. 'Let's get out of here.'

They left the pen, locking the gate behind them, and peeped through the slits in the bamboo screen.

The wolf struggled to his feet and looked around, blinking. Then he sat down suddenly as if he was dizzy.

I know how you feel, Jake thought sympathetically.

They watched the wolf for a few minutes more until Gite was satisfied that he'd be all right. 'Poor Ras,' she said. 'He's probably very confused.'

'Ras? Is that his name?' asked Shani.

'Yes. He's named after Ras Dejen, the highest peak in Ethiopia. We've named all the wolves after mountains,' Gite explained. 'Mainly mountains in this country.'

'Why mountains?' said Jake.

'Cause that's where the wolves live,' said Shani at once. 'Sheesh, you're slow, Jake.'

Jake could only nod. With his pounding headache, the nausea and the dizziness, he certainly wasn't at his brightest. But he didn't want to make a fuss. He'd be fine in the morning after a good night's sleep – and no more coffee. *Maybe I'll even have a nap now,* he decided, hoping that everyone else would just sit around until it was supper time.

He was wrong.

'I'll see if I can get something for Ras to eat,' said Celia when they reached the rondavels. They went inside where Gite began to prepare a pot of coffee.

'I'll help you feed Ras,' Shani said to Celia. 'I bet you'd like to as well, Jake,' she added.

'Sure,' Jake said automatically. He was torn between trying to sleep off whatever was making him feel so ill and doing something to help Ras.

Celia gave them both an amused look. 'You might take back your offer when you hear what's involved.'

'No, we won't,' Jake said. 'We've even fed a lioness before.' That had to be more tricky than feeding an Ethiopian Wolf. The lioness Jake was thinking about had been kept in an enclosure in Musabi with her two cubs while they were being filmed. The producer had been dead set on keeping the cubs as pets, but eventually agreed to let them go as long as he could get some footage of them with their mother.

'That lioness was really savage,' Shani put in. 'You should have seen how she tore into the meat we threw over the fence.'

'That's not exactly how we'll be feeding Ras,' said Celia. 'You see, he prefers his food to be fresh which is why Bedassa and I have to go out hunting.'

'Hunting for what?' Shani frowned.

'Grass-rats and moles,' Celia announced. 'We look for their burrows then, like the wolves, wait for them to pop out. It seems cruel, I know, but it's all part of caring for the wolves. Still want to help?'

'Er, yes,' said Shani, less eagerly than before, while Jake nodded. He didn't relish the idea of trapping live rats, but he'd do it if it was important for Ras.

But Gabriel had something else planned for them. 'Perhaps you can go rat hunting tomorrow,' he said. 'We need to go out on our mules again today before it gets dark.'

Jake groaned inwardly. Another trek on the stubborn Emperor was the last thing on earth he felt like right now. 'Where are we going?'

'We want to check on a den just up the mountain,' said Gite, pouring the piping hot black liquid into tin mugs. 'Oh, and put on something warm before we go. It gets icy cold here the minute the sun sinks behind the mountains.'

Jake burrowed into the depths of his rucksack for

a fleece and pulled it on. Gite, Gabriel and Shani finished their coffee then put on warm jackets too.

'Before we go, have a look at this map,' said Gabriel. He spread it out on the floor in front of Jake and Shani. 'It'll give you some idea of where the wolves are.'

The map showed the mountainous area around Abuna Joseph. Gabriel pointed out the territories of the four wolf packs. 'This is where the River family live,' he said, circling an area that included a narrow thread of blue. 'And here to the west is the Cliff family. Then up in the north where the mountain gets really steep is the Ridge clan. The last group is quite close to us, just a bit further up the mountain on a plateau. That's where we're headed now.'

'Let me guess,' said Shani. 'They're the Plateau group.'

'That's right,' said Gite.

'Sounds like a group of singers,' chuckled Shani.

'I think you're getting them mixed up with The Platters,' Jake said remembering a CD that his gran had in England.

Gite grinned. 'Wolves can sing, too. You'll hear them sooner or later.'

They went to fetch their mules, meeting up with Mengistu again.

'It's very bad news about the wolf,' the minder remarked solemnly. 'And unfortunate for our young visitors to see such terrible things.'

'Oh, but we haven't come to sightsee,' Shani reminded the man. 'We've come to help, even if there is rabies around.'

Riding in single file, and with Emperor on his best behaviour for a change, they set out from the camp, following a track that passed near the quarantine pen. Jake caught a glimpse of Ras pacing beside the fence as if he was trying to find a way out. 'He looks so lonely,' he murmured.

'Yes, that's probably going to be the hardest part for him,' said Gite. 'Ethiopian wolves are very social. They sleep close together and meet up several times a day. They're usually only alone when they're hunting.'

The track led them up the rocky slope to a small grass-covered area. Despite feeling rough, Jake was excited about checking on the den and seeing a wolf in the wild. Perhaps quite a few of the Plateau clan would be there.

Reaching the plateau, Gabriel and Gite slid off their mules and tethered them to a lobelia tree. 'We'll go the rest of the way on foot,' said Gabriel.

Jake and Shani dismounted too and Jake looked around for somewhere to tether Emperor. There were no other trees for miles around and the shrubs were all too small. One tug from a strong mule and they'd be uprooted.

'It's OK,' said Mengistu, taking the reins from Jake. 'I'll stay here with the mules. You go on to the den.'

'Thanks,' said Jake.

He and Shani followed Gabriel and Gite across the grass towards a rocky outcrop. When they were about twenty-five metres away, Gabriel put his finger to his lips. 'Sssh,' he whispered, veering sideways into some boulders.

'Over there,' he breathed when they were safely hidden. 'Beneath that overhang.'

The sun was sinking fast now so that long shadows darkened the plateau. For a while, Jake could see nothing in the half-light but suddenly a tiny movement caught his eye. In an instant, he forgot his nausea and headache as he made out a little heap of dark grey bodies curled up tightly together.

It was a litter of wolf pups!

FIVE

'I think I can see four,' Jake whispered. He glanced at Gite. 'Did you know about them?'

'Oh yes. They're two weeks old already and we've been checking on them just about every day since they were born.'

'They're gorgeous,' breathed Shani.

Gite smiled. 'We thought you'd fall in love with them.'

'And it's good that you can see something good after all the bad news about rabies and poor Ras coming in looking so miserable,' added Gabriel.

'I thought he looked great,' Jake said loyally.

The pups began to stir, and one of them lifted its head and blinked at Jake. Jake saw that it had the same long muzzle and pointed ears as Ras. 'But their coats are a different colour,' he observed quietly.

'That'll change quite soon,' said Gabriel. 'When they're about three weeks old. That's when they'll start leaving the den, too.'

'Where's their mother?' Shani asked, looking around.

'Probably still out hunting. But she'll be back by dark,' said Gite.

'What's her name?' said Jake.

'Etna.'

'*Edna!* That sounds like someone's old aunt, not a wolf,' protested Shani. 'I don't know of any mountains called that.'

Gabriel chuckled softly. 'I must get my English pronunciation right. It's Etna, not Edna.'

'Like Mount Etna?' Jake suggested.

'But that's not in Ethiopia,' Shani objected.

Gabriel smiled at her. 'You're quite right. It's a volcano in Sicily. But we chose it as a symbolic name. You see, we're hoping that in time, the wolves will increase so much that we run out of names of Ethiopian mountains. Then we'll have to choose mountains in other parts of the world.'

'So, Etna's sort of paving the way,' Jake remarked.

They watched the pups for a while then Gite said it was time to go. 'We don't want to upset Etna when she comes back.' She turned and started back towards Mengistu and the mules.

Jake was reluctant to leave. The cubs were wide awake now, whining and sniffing about as if they were hungry. He hated it when baby animals were left alone in their dens or nests, even though he knew this was very common among predators who had to go hunting for food. But seeing the defenceless wolf pups brought back memories of a litter of cheetah cubs that he and Shani had been watching. A male lion had suddenly appeared and killed two of the cubs. The third, a rare King Cheetah cub that Jake and Shani named Cheepard, had only survived by hiding in a crack in the rocks.

'The cubs will be fine in their den,' Gabriel reassured Jake as if he'd read his mind. 'It's outside that they'll confront the real dangers.'

'Like other predators?' Jake said.

'That certainly, and of course rabies. Their habitat is also a big problem,' explained Gabriel. 'These animals can live only in the Afro-alpine regions of this country and unless those areas are conserved, there will be nowhere for the Ethiopian Wolf to go.'

Jake remembered the cultivated fields he'd seen yesterday on the trek up from Lalibela. They covered so much of the land and had already crept far up the mountain slopes.

'There's more though,' put in Gite. 'Inter-breeding with domestic dogs is a major problem because the offspring are hybrids which are much more vulnerable to disease and birth defects.'

Shani glanced back towards the den. 'I hope Etna's pups aren't hybrids.'

'No. Those are pure-bred Ethiopian Wolves,' said Gabriel with a smile. 'We're pretty sure their father is the Plateau group's alpha male, a magnificent chap called Darkeena. He's a lot like his father, Tullu, the wolf we told you about yesterday.'

'Will we see Darkeena?' Jake asked, looking across the plateau.

'I hope so. The Plateau pack's home range is very small, only about three square kilometres,' said Gabriel. 'But the wolves are quite timid, so I can't say for sure you'll see any of them. Still, we usually hear them when we patrol the range.'

'How often do you do that?' asked Shani.

'Bedassa comes up here almost every day,' said Gite. 'To check for poison.'

'Poison?' Jake echoed in dismay.

'Yes. Another threat to the wolves, I'm afraid,' said Gite. 'Farmers leave poisoned meat lying around. It's meant for hyenas, but the wolves sometimes take it.'

Another wave of nausea welled up in Jake. He couldn't believe people could leave poison lying around that might be eaten by the threatened wolf population.

They came to the mules and he leaned against Emperor, trying to get his breath back. He felt a sudden rush of affection for the animal which stood utterly still, almost as if he knew Jake needed a bit of support. 'Thanks, pal,' he murmured.

Mengistu looked at him with concern. 'You look ill,' he said.

'I'm fine,' Jake insisted.

'Are you sure?' Shani put a hand on his arm.

'Yes,' Jake said, feeling irritated again. 'Just leave me alone.' He bent over, his hands resting on his knees, trying to take some deep breaths. 'It's just that I hate to think of animals being poisoned. It's not their fault they can't find anything but sheep to eat.' He shivered as a gust of icy wind blew up the mountain slope. Gita was right. With the sun disappearing behind the mountains, the temperature was dropping rapidly.

'The farmers probably don't see it that way,' said Shani, doing up the zip of her jacket. Having lived in a rural village all her life, she could usually see both sides when animals and humans came into conflict. 'To them, hyenas are a pest.'

'I suppose so,' Jake admitted. 'But people can't just go round poisoning animals, especially when rare animals might end up being killed too.' As if on cue, the spine tingling howl of a hyena suddenly pierced the early evening stillness. And then came another howl, different from the hyena's chortling call.

Gita was sitting on her mule. She put up her hand. 'Wolf,' she said, just as Jake saw the jackal-like shape of an Ethiopian Wolf standing on a rock in the middle of the plateau.

'We're in luck after all,' he breathed.

The animal lifted its face to the sky and howled again.

The haunting sound rang out across the hills as it must have done for thousands of years. 'It sounds so sad,' Shani whispered, and Jake found himself wondering how much longer the world would hear the beautiful cry.

'They can't become extinct,' he said with feeling.

The wolf stopped howling and looked around.

'Do you recognize that one?' Shani asked Gite.

'It's Darkeena.'

'The pup's father,' said Shani, her eyes shining. 'Now we only need to see Etna and we've met the whole family.'

Darkeena sprang down from the rock and trotted across the plateau, his bushy white and black tail swaying behind him. When he came to a tree he sniffed around it then sprayed the trunk before moving on to the next tree.

Shani laughed. 'He looks like my dog Bweha!'

'Yes, marking his territory like most animals do,' said Gabriel. 'The others in the group might join him soon – maybe even Etna on her way back to the den. The pack often gathers just before sunset.'

Darkeena looked back over his shoulder, his sharp gaze falling on Jake, before he flicked his tail and ran into the distance.

'Wow,' Jake murmured, a tingle running up his spine.

With his red coat matching the glow of the setting sun, Darkeena soon merged into the background and all Jake could see of him was an occasional white flash when his tail caught the fading sun's rays. In the east, the sky had turned a rich violet colour as night began to creep across the mountains.

'We must hurry now,' said Gite. 'Soon we won't be able to see in front of us.'

Jake glanced at his watch. It was nearly six o'clock. Just twelve hours ago, they'd set out from Lalibela. *What a day it's been*, he thought as he climbed on to Emperor. After what Gabriel and Gite had told him about the conservation programme, he had expected that he and Shani would be spending a lot of time analysing droppings and going walkabout to ask people to vaccinate their dogs. Who'd have thought that they'd have already handled a wolf, seen a litter of pups at close quarters, and found themselves caught up in a rabies crisis?

They hadn't gone far when Jake's keen eyes picked out another wolf foraging among a pile of rocks not far away. The wolf must have been upwind from them because it seemed unaware they were there. Jake silently pointed it out to the others and they all stopped to watch.

'That's Etna,' said Gabriel and Jake saw the swollen teats that indicated that the wolf was nursing pups.

'Now we *have* seen the whole family,' Shani whispered triumphantly.

Etna was sniffing and licking something so that Jake assumed she'd made a kill. 'It looks like she's caught a rat,' he said.

Still oblivious to its human audience, the wolf

started to tuck in to its meal. *This is just brilliant*, Jake thought.

But his delight quickly turned to confusion when Gabriel suddenly cried out, 'No!'

'What is it?'

'That's no rat. It looks like bait!' Gite gasped.

'No, Etna,' Gabriel yelled so loudly that the wolf looked up at him then turned and ran across the plateau.

Gite stared helplessly after her. 'Please don't let her have eaten it,' she prayed.

Gabriel jumped off his mule at once and ran over to where Etna had been. Even though he was still struggling to breathe normally, Jake followed. They hunted about the rocks, hoping that Etna had been so startled by Gabriel's shout that she'd abandoned the meat.

They found nothing.

'She might have taken it back to her pups,' Jake suggested, feeling his stomach churn with horror.

'They're not weaned yet. That only starts when they're five weeks old,' said Gabriel. 'Whatever it was, she's eaten it,' he concluded, his eyes sparking with anger.

'So what do we do now?' Jake asked. 'Go after her?'

'We could, but she'll hide herself away if she knows we're after her. Also it'll be dark soon,' said Gabriel. 'We'll have to go back to camp and go out looking for her first thing in the morning.'

With the light fading fast, they trotted back to camp. All the way, Jake thought about Etna. *And there's Ras as well, so that's two wolves in serious danger in just one day.*

It was almost dark by the time they rode back into camp. Celia and Bedassa were waiting for them outside the main rondavel. 'We thought something had happened to you,' said Celia.

'Not to us. But to Etna,' Gabriel responded grimly then explained what had happened.

'Maybe it wasn't bait,' said Celia, trying to sound positive. 'It could have been a rat that Etna caught among the rocks.'

'Could have been,' Gabriel agreed, 'except that I saw a herdsman leaving some bait in the same place just last week. I picked it up of course, but he might have left a fresh piece.'

Bedassa and Mengistu led the mules to their pen and Jake and the others went inside the rondavel. Two paraffin lanterns provided a soft light, and a coal stove gave off some welcome heat. Shani stood in front of it to warm her hands and asked the question that everyone seemed to have been avoiding. 'If it was poison, and Etna dies, what'll happen to the pups?'

'There's another adult female in the Plateau group,' said Gite, taking off her anorak and joining Shani in front of the stove. 'Her name's Guna. We'd have to hope she'd take over and raise them.'

'And if she doesn't?' Jake pressed. 'Would you hand-rear them?' He knew that hand-rearing wild animals was thought of as interfering in nature, one of Jake's pet subjects. But this wasn't a natural situation at all. And sometimes orphaned animals just had to be rescued. *Like when Rick and I took Bina home*, Jake thought. Usually, Rick would have turned away to let nature takes its course, but when the eagle grabbed Bina's mother right in front of his eyes, he was as moved as Jake by the helpless little antelope.

But having grown up among humans, Bina would never be able to survive in the wild on her own. Was this the kind of life the wolf pups would have to lead?

'I'm not so sure about hand-rearing them,' Gabriel said, putting a pot of water on the stove to make some tea. 'It's not our plan to have any wolves in captivity. We'll just have to hope Celia's guess is right and that it was a rat Etna found. We'll ride up to the den again in the morning to see if the pups are OK.'

Jake knew he wouldn't sleep a wink before then, and when he caught Shani's eye, he guessed that she felt the same way. 'I just wish we could have done something to help,' Shani said miserably.

Gite put a hand on her shoulder. 'It's a harsh world out there,' she said.

Jake lay down on his sleeping bag and stared up at the ceiling. The trip he'd been so excited about was turning into a nightmare and he half-wished he was back home, unaware of the tragedies unfolding in the Ethiopian highlands.

Gite must have sensed his despair. 'Good things happen too,' she said, then, changing the subject, she added, 'I think you and Shani should phone your parents to let them know you've arrived safely. They're probably as worried about you as you are about the wolves.'

'They can't be,' Jake murmured.

There was a satellite phone in the camp so he and Shani made brief calls home. Jake told Rick and Hannah about the dramas in the wolf community but kept quiet about how sick he felt. He couldn't handle his mum getting anxious over the phone.

When supper arrived, Jake couldn't eat a thing. The nausea and his anxiety over Ras and Etna and her pups made him want to throw up at the sight of the food on his plate.

Shani had no appetite either, and pushed the food around her plate with her spoon.

'It's much tastier than it looks,' Celia tried to encourage them. 'It's called shiro,' she added, dipping her spoon into the mush of lentils and chickpeas. There was more injera too, as well as bottled water.

They were sitting on low stools in one of the rondavels, their plates on their laps. Mengistu was strumming a guitar that he'd brought with him and the gentle music made Jake begin to feel sleepy. He looked up and saw that Gite was watching him.

'You really don't look at all well, Jake,' she remarked. 'Do you still have that headache?'

Jake nodded.

'And nausea?'

'Yeah, I feel pretty sick most of the time.'

'He can't breathe properly either,' put in Shani. Jake frowned at her. The last thing he wanted was a lot of attention.

'You know what I think?' said Gite.

Jake shook his head.

'You've got altitude sickness.'

'I have? What's that?' With the way things were going, Jake wouldn't have been surprised to hear that it was a really serious disease.

'It's when your body battles to adapt to a higher altitude because there's less oxygen in the air,' Gabriel explained. 'It's a horrible thing, I know, but you'll be OK in a day or two.'

Just knowing what was wrong with him made Jake feel a whole lot better, but nothing could take away the desperation he felt for the pups and their mother.

'I think you should stay in camp tomorrow and try to rest while we go and check the den,' suggested Gite.

Jake looked at her aghast. 'No way!' Nothing in the world would prevent him from going to see if the pups and Etna were all right.

SIX

Please let Etna be there. Please let Etna be there. Like a mantra, Jake repeated the words over and over again to himself during the nail-biting ride to the den the next morning.

He was still feeling sick and breathless, even though he had managed to get more sleep than he expected last night. For a few seconds early this morning when he was awoken by an arrow of sun shining into his eyes, he couldn't remember where he was. He'd sat up and looked around, then saw Shani sitting in her sleeping bag opposite him, writing in her diary. As a feeling of nausea gripped him, everything had come flooding back and his next thoughts were of Ras and Etna and her pups.

After breakfast, which like supper the night before, Jake couldn't touch, he and Shani had gone with Gite to check on Ras. The wolf saw them coming and darted behind some rocks but all the same Gite thought he looked OK and that his wound wasn't any worse.

57

They'd gone back to the rondavels to get ready for their trek up to the plateau and found Gabriel on the phone. 'It's Born Free,' he told Gite, putting his hand over the receiver. 'I thought they should know about the rabies. They want to know if there's anything they can do to help.'

'Born Free? That's a movie, isn't it?' said Shani.

'Yes, but it's also a foundation that works to save wild animals,' Gite explained. 'The co-founders starred in the movie and were so moved by the lions and other wildlife that they met while filming, they decided to set up a pioneering animal charity. They're our sponsors so they're very closely involved with what goes on here.'

With Gite and Gabriel busy with the important phone call, and Bedassa hunting for rats for Ras, Celia was in charge of leading the trek up to the plateau. Mengistu was at the back as usual, whistling softly.

He sounds cheerful this morning, Jake thought, wondering for about the hundredth time why he and Shani needed to be followed like this. *It's not like we're criminals*, he thought.

They came to the plateau and dismounted. Mengistu offered to look after the mules and his horse again while Jake, Shani and Celia checked on the den. They came to the heap of rocks and ducked behind them to peer across to the overhang.

'Oh, look,' Shani whispered. 'They're awake!'

The four pups were stumbling about and whining as if they were very hungry.

Jake's heart dropped to his boots. Etna couldn't have come back. If she had, surely the pups would be sleeping contentedly with their bellies full? He glanced at Celia, his eyes wide.

Celia shrugged. 'They look OK,' she whispered, answering his unspoken question. 'But they're obviously hungry.'

A gust of wind blew against Jake and he realized that it was blowing over them, towards the den. Perhaps Etna had picked up their scent and run away.

Just then, out of the corner of his eye, he glimpsed a fleeting movement to one side of the overhang. He focussed his gaze and felt a shiver of excitement when he saw a wolf half-hidden behind a rock. The animal was watching them suspiciously, the look on its face reminding Jake of a timid dog. *It's got to be Etna*, he thought.

He nudged Celia, and with a tiny nod, pointed out the wolf to her. 'Etna?' he mouthed.

Celia shook her head. 'The other female,' she said very quietly. 'Guna.'

'Why's she hanging about the den?' asked Shani so softly that Jake had to lip-read to make out what she was saying.

Celia looked unhappy. 'Possibly to suckle Etna's cubs.'

Jake felt as if he'd been winded. So Etna couldn't

have made it home. A horrible picture came into his mind of Etna, curled up in agony as she died from the poison.

Eventually Celia said, 'I guess we might as well go back. If Etna is OK, she might be out hunting, and if she isn't . . . ' Her voice trailed off.

'Can't we go looking for her?' Jake pleaded.

'Yes, we'll scour the plateau until we find her,' Celia said firmly. 'But you must prepare yourselves for the worst,' she warned.

'At least the pups aren't completely alone,' said Shani, for Guna was still there, watching over the litter as if it was her own.

They crept out of the shelter and started back toward the mules. Halfway there, a tiny noise behind them made Jake turn round.

Guna was standing in front of the den watching the three humans walking away, and standing next to her was another wolf. A nursing mother, Jake saw at once.

'Etna!' he exclaimed, in a hoarse whisper.

Shani and Celia spun round, their faces breaking into broad smiles when they saw the mother wolf.

'That's her all right,' Celia confirmed. 'She couldn't have taken the poison after all.'

Jake was so relieved, he could have shouted out to the mountain tops that all was well for the little family and that one more precious wolf hadn't been lost to the world.

Heartened, but resolving to keep an eye open for poisoned bait on the way back to camp, the three returned to Mengistu.

'Everything's OK,' Jake told the government official, who gave one of his rare smiles and said, 'Ah, so I have some excellent news to report to my department,' which made Jake wonder exactly what Mengistu told his bosses about him and Shani.

'It's probably the best thing that's happened since we arrived,' smiled Shani, patting her mule, Angel.

'That's for sure,' Jake agreed. And then something else dawned on him. He'd been too tense to notice before, but he was breathing a lot easier and wasn't feeling nauseous. His headache had faded too, so that he hardly noticed it. 'Hey!' he exclaimed. 'I'm better. The altitude sickness has gone.'

'Then you'd probably say yes to one of these,' said Celia, taking some bananas out of her backpack.

'Yes, please,' said Jake.

They climbed up a steep bank and sat down on a wide ledge to have their picnic. Far below, the Wollo foothills looked green and lush in the clear morning sun. Jake could see the tiny figures of sheep herders tending their flocks which, from such a height, were no more than pinpricks of white and black moving slowly across the hillsides.

'It's so peaceful up here,' remarked Shani. She looked around at the towering reaches of the mountains. 'Is that an eagle?' she said, pointing into the sky at a huge bird with a wingspan that must have been several times the length of its body. Effortlessly, the great bird soared higher and higher on unseen thermals.

'It's a Bearded Vulture,' Celia told her. 'Lammergeier is its more common name. And, like the wolves, it's becoming increasingly rare.'

'What else lives up here?' Jake asked.

Celia took out some bottles of water and gave one each to Jake and Shani as well as to Mengistu.

The minder took a sip of water and said, 'Leopards live up here. Some people say there are Abyssinian lions too.'

'Sheesh!' remarked Shani, looking around. 'I hope one doesn't creep up on us.'

Celia chuckled. 'That's highly unlikely. I've never seen a lion in all the time I've been here.'

Shani looked relieved but there was still a flicker of anxiety in her eyes. Jake knew what was troubling her. After the lion had attacked the cheetah cubs in Musabi, it had turned on Jake and Shani. They'd managed to scramble into a tree only seconds before the angry cat got to them. It was a narrow escape that Jake would never forget, and he was pretty certain Shani wouldn't either. Still, he wouldn't mind seeing an Abyssinian lion, but from a safe distance.

Celia took the cap off her bottle and took a swig. 'There are also a few other special animals in these mountains,' she said. 'Like the walia ibex.'

Shani frowned. 'The *what*?'

'Walia ibex,' Celia repeated with a grin. 'It's a wild goat that has a beard and thick curved horns.'

'There's one over there,' said Mengistu, pointing to a ridge in the west.

'That's miles away,' said Shani, looking in that direction. 'How can you see anything there?'

'Practised eyes,' Mengistu said, baring his teeth in a smile.

'Oh,' said Jake, feeling slightly uncomfortable. Mengistu was nice, but he could be really creepy sometimes. He started at the ridge and thought he saw something move. But the harder he looked, the less he actually saw.

'We should have brought our binoculars,' said Shani.

'Never mind,' said Celia. 'You're bound to see one more closely. Something else you'll probably see are Gelada Baboons, or lion monkeys. Like the wolves, they're only found in the Ethiopian highlands.'

'We call them bleeding-heart baboons,' Mengistu added. 'Because of the patch of red heart-shaped skin on their chests.'

'You'll hear them before you see them,' said Celia. 'They're very vocal and they move around in huge troops, sometimes up to a hundred animals.'

'That must be awesome,' said Jake. 'We've got baboons in Musabi but the troops aren't anything as big as that.'

Celia stood up, gathering the water bottles and putting them in her rucksack. 'Time to be getting back. I have some paperwork to do before we go out on patrol to check on the River pack later today. And we'd like you two to capture some data on Gabriel's laptop. We're so busy that we battle to keep up with things like that. We'd also like you to prepare for a school visit on Monday, and, if you're not too squeamish, come out looking for rats for Ras.'

'Will do,' Shani said cheerfully. She waved her hand to indicate that she needed to slip behind a bush for a moment so the others went ahead, walking slowly to give her a chance to catch up.

Jake kept thinking of Etna's pups. 'Do they have names yet?' he asked Celia.

'Not yet. Perhaps you and Shani would like to help us choose some for them.'

'Yes, please,' said Jake. 'We'll have to look at an atlas to see what other mountains there are in this country.' Thinking that the team must soon start running out of local names for the pups, he asked if any others had been born in the past few days.

'Not yet, but we're expecting one or two litters in the next week or so,' Celia said. 'The alpha River female is pregnant, and we think the Ridge family is expecting a litter too.'

'So many all at the same time,' Jake remarked. 'That's good news.'

'Yes it is,' she agreed. 'But not every female breeds

successfully every year, and those that do give birth only in the dry season, which is now.'

Looking down to the green valleys, Jake found it hard to believe it was the dry season. From what he'd read about the highlands of Ethiopia before he came here, he knew the rains had finished only a few weeks ago in early October.

He glanced over his shoulder to see if Shani had reappeared yet. She was just passing the ledge where they'd all sat for their picnic. 'Hurry up, slowcoach,' he called to her.

At that same moment he saw an animal leap out from behind a rock higher up the slope. Without breaking its stride, it ran down the hill towards Shani.

For a split second, Jake thought it was another wolf, but then he realized that it couldn't be. It was dark and scrawny and much bigger than a wolf. Snarling savagely, it hurtled closer and closer to Shani, who hadn't seen it yet.

Pure terror flooded Jake, almost paralysing him. 'Look out!' he managed to shout, the words coming out in a strangled squeak. He started scrambling up the slope, but Celia grabbed his shirt and yanked him back.

'Run!' she yelled, pushing Jake down the steep bank in front of her. Then she screamed at the top of her voice to Shani, 'Run as fast as you can!'

SEVEN

Jake saw Shani break into a rapid jog; he took off as well, half-running, half-sliding down the path. 'Run, Shani,' he yelled, without understanding what was happening. All he knew was that it had to be serious.

He heard Celia shout something to Mengistu who had almost reached the mules. The man stopped in his tracks and looked round, his eyes opening wide with alarm.

'What's going on?' Jake called.

'Get away from that dog,' shouted Mengistu. 'It's rabid!'

Rabid! A feeling of terror like none he'd ever known before raced through Jake. But the terror was for Shani, not for himself. 'Shani!' he screamed. He whirled round and saw his friend skidding in panic down the hill, the maddened animal only metres behind. And then, like it was happening in slow motion, he saw her stumble and fall.

'Get up!' Jake cried, fear clutching his heart.

But the dog caught Shani up in a few quick strides.

Foaming at the mouth, it lunged at her, sinking its teeth into the back of her leg.

Shani screamed, a bloodcurdling cry that slammed into the mountains then ricocheted back to echo through the hills and valleys. She struggled to get away, but the dog clung on, bracing its front paws against the ground.

'Get off her!' Jake yelled and he tore back up the slope.

'Come back,' Celia shouted. 'You'll get bitten too.'

Jake didn't care. He had to help Shani.

There was a brief movement behind him, then, 'Get down, Jake,' warned Celia, and this time she meant it. Jake instinctively threw himself to one side as an ear-splitting crack rang out. The dog slumped to the ground, and Shani's frightened sobs broke through the gunshot ringing in Jake's ears.

He looked back and saw Mengistu lowering a pistol to his side. Then he pushed himself to his feet and bounded up the hill to his friend.

Shani was lying in a crumpled heap, crying uncontrollably. Blood pumped out of the jagged bite wound on her calf.

The dog lay beside her, its desperate rage stilled forever.

Jake knelt down and put his arms around Shani. 'It's OK. It's OK,' he said. He rummaged in his pocket and found a crumpled tissue. He started to dab the wound but Celia shook her head as she appeared beside him, her long blonde hair escaping from its plait.

'Don't,' she said. 'It's better if the blood keeps flowing.'

She took out the water bottles and poured what was left on to the wound. 'If only we had some antiseptic,' she said. 'That would help to reduce the risk.'

Shani looked up at Celia, her eyes wide with fear. 'Risk?' she echoed in a small, frightened voice. 'Do you mean, a risk from r . . . r . . . rabies?'

Celia nodded and for a moment Jake felt the ground sway as if he was going to be sick.

To Jake's surprise, Shani sat up and said calmly, 'That means I need a vaccine fast.' She looked at Celia. 'Will you take me to the nearest hospital, please?'

'Of course,' said Celia. 'But first we must clean that wound as much as possible.'

'I know,' agreed Shani, and gasped as she looked at the bite for the first time. 'I'm going to need stitches.' She winced in pain then looked away. 'And antibiotics. Also an anti-tetanus shot.'

Celia raised her eyebrows. 'You've just been bitten by a dog that's probably rabid and you're discussing the treatment you need!'

'My mum's a nurse,' Shani explained through gritted teeth. 'And I've always understood about rabies, ever since I was very little. As long as I get vaccinated soon and the bite doesn't get infected, I'll be OK.'

Her words were brave, but a quiver in her voice gave away the fear she must have been feeling. And although she tried to smile, her eyes were wide and her face an unnaturally ashen colour.

Jake tried to stay positive for her sake. Below, by the mules, Mengistu was talking into a radio and Jake guessed he was reporting the incident, either to the authorities or to Gite and Gabriel.

At least there are people there likely to help us, he thought, and then, out loud, he said to Shani, 'You'll be back at camp and vaccinated before you know it.'

'Let's get you up,' said Celia, and she and Jake helped Shani to her feet.

But Shani's legs buckled beneath her. 'It hurts too much,' she sobbed, collapsing on the ground.

'I'll give you a piggy-back,' Jake said, crouching down to help her on to his back.

'Sure you can manage?' Celia asked him, and glanced at Mengistu who'd finished talking over the radio and was coming up the hill to help.

'Positive,' said Jake who'd have carried his best friend down the mountain even if she weighed three times as much as she did. 'And don't worry about a thing, Shani. I'll make sure you're OK,' he promised. Tears welled up in his eyes but with his arms supporting Shani, he couldn't wipe them away. He blinked and sniffed, and suddenly it was Shani's turn to comfort him.

'You mustn't worry either, Jake,' she said, touching him lightly on his cheek.

They started down the hill again, Jake treading carefully to avoid tripping and hurting Shani further.

Mangistu reached them. 'This should never have happened,' he said with such feeling that Jake wondered if the man had disapproved of him and Shani coming to this remote place all along. 'I will carry her for you,' the minder added.

Jake shook his head. 'I can manage.'

Even though he was frantic with worry over his best friend, he also felt a shudder of fear for the wolves of Abuna Joseph. Had any of them encountered the dog too? Was this the same one that had bitten Ras? He glanced back at the lifeless body and felt pity for it too, but at least it was now out of its misery. It probably wouldn't have lived much longer, but in that short time, Jake knew it would have suffered horribly. He'd seen terrifying photographs in Mrs Rafiki's clinic of dogs in the final stages of the disease. Driven mad by thirst, frothing at the mouth and often paralysed, they looked as if they'd landed in hell.

When they reached the mules and horses, Shani said she'd be able to ride Angel back, but Mengistu wouldn't hear of it. 'It will be better if you sit on my horse in front of me,' he said. Lifting her off Jake's back, he hoisted her gently into the saddle then pulled himself up behind her, his arms curved round her waist.

'What about Angel?' Shani asked fretfully.

'I'll look after her,' said Jake, taking Angel's reins and leading her over to Emperor.

Mengistu made a clicking sound and said something in his language, and the big black horse immediately broke into a canter.

Jake swung himself on to Emperor's back. 'No playing up this time, please,' he begged, but the warning was unnecessary for the mule set off at a willing trot with Angel next to him and Celia at the back.

With the horse easily outpacing the mules, Mengistu and Shani were quickly out of sight and Jake was glad that his friend would soon be back at camp where Gite would probably be able to give her the treatment she needed.

Jake and Celia were about halfway to the camp when they saw Bedassa coming toward them. 'Mengistu radioed the camp about the attack,' he said. 'Where exactly is the dog?'

Celia told him where to find it. 'He's going to fetch the dog so that we can take a sample of brain tissue to have it tested for rabies,' she explained to Jake.

By the time they rode in to camp, Shani was lying on her sleeping bag in the main rondavel. Gite and Gabriel were crouching next to her, their faces drawn with worry. The open first-aid kit was on a stool next to them. Mengistu was on the other side of the room talking to someone on the satellite phone.

'We're going to have to get you down to Lalibela,' said Gite, applying an antiseptic ointment to the wound before giving Shani a painkilling injection.

'But that's an eight hour trek!' Jake gasped. 'You can't expect Shani to go all that way.'

'I'm sorry, but it's where the nearest hospital is,' said Gabriel.

'Don't you have any vaccine here?' Jake asked desperately.

'Only for canines,' Celia told him. She wrapped a clean bandage around Shani's leg. 'We usually have human vaccine too, but it expired about a week ago and we've been waiting for fresh stock from Addis.'

Jake could hardly believe his ears.

'It's OK,' Shani said weakly. She must have seen the distress on his face. 'I'll be fine, as long as I get to hospital and have the treatment.'

'We'll head back down as soon as we have the brain specimens,' said Gabriel. 'Mengistu is making arrangements for it to be flown from Lalibela to the state vet in Addis.'

Before long, Jake heard the thundering of a horse's hooves. He looked out and saw Bedassa galloping into camp, the dog wrapped in plastic and, like Ras's first appearance, draped across the saddle in front of him. Only this time, the animal was dead.

Bedassa continued past the rondavels to a small shed on the far side of the camp. Celia put on some protective clothing which included gloves, a plastic apron, gumboots and a visor, then went to remove the brain tissue.

Meanwhile, Jake and the others prepared for the return trek to Lalibela. They packed some warm clothes for Shani in case it should turn cold, as well as food and water. Most importantly, Gite made sure the first-aid kit contained more painkillers.

Finally, leaving Celia and Bedassa to look after Ras, Jake and the others set out for Lalibela. Mengistu was carrying the brain tissue in his saddle bag. The specimens had been secured in a screw-cap jar before being sealed in two plastic bags and packed in a firm cardboard box.

Once again, Mengistu insisted that Shani sat on his saddle in front of him. 'That's the best way I can take care of you,' he said, and Jake began to understand that the minder really had been assigned to them to make sure they were safe.

The torturous journey back down the mountain seemed a lot longer than the trek up from Lalibela. More children than before ran alongside, their high-pitched voices no longer amusing to Jake but instead intensely irritating as they begged for 'birr' and pens.

Mengistu folded his arms more securely around Shani and shooed the children away, but they quickly came back.

'Can't you see Shani's been bitten?' Jake cried out impatiently but the children couldn't understand him and merely gaped at the bandage on Shani's leg.

Even more frustrating than the children was the livestock that kept wandering across the track, blocking the path and slowing the journey up. Jake had to stop himself from shouting in rage. 'We're never going to get there,' he muttered more than once.

Once a large ox refused to budge and there was no way round it because the sides of the path rose up sheer. The enormous beast stood in the middle of the track, chewing the cud and staring at the mules and their riders.

'Move!' shouted Gabriel, waving his arms. 'Out of the way.'

Unperturbed, the ox gazed at him from heavy-lidded eyes.

'Hey, you! Move!' Jake yelled. He looked at Shani sitting in front of Mengistu. Her head was lolling and Jake guessed the painkiller was making her drowsy. Either that, or she was passing out from pain and shock.

'Move!' he shouted at the top of his voice so that Shani looked up, startled.

In the end it was Gite who managed to get the beast to budge. She dismounted and, picking up a stick, tapped the ox on its rump to herd it along the track. As soon as the path widened out, she persuaded it to stand to one side and allow the mules and Mengistu's horse to pass.

Eventually, late in the afternoon, and with Jake's nerves worn to a shred, they rode into Lalibela and clattered along the busy street that led to the hospital. It was the very one they'd taken yesterday, never dreaming that they'd soon be back.

In the dusty yard outside the small building that looked more like a clinic than a proper hospital, Jake leapt off Emperor and ran round to help Shani down from Mengistu's horse.

Gabriel was right behind him. 'Let me,' he said and scooped Shani up in his arms, then carried her effortlessly inside.

Mengistu wheeled his horse around and rode out of the yard. He was going straight to his office where someone was waiting to take the brain sample to the airport.

Expecting their ordeal to be almost over, Jake had a major shock when he went through the door. Even though it was late in the day, the tiny hospital was chock-a-block with sick and injured people. The few seats in the waiting room were taken, and there was barely space to stand in the cramped area. A few people, too ill to stay on their feet, sat on the floor with their backs against the walls.

'Isn't there another hospital?' Jake blurted out. 'Or a doctor's surgery? It'll be hours before Shani's seen.'

'I hope not,' Gite said grimly. 'This is the only

hospital in Lalibela so we're going to have to wait like everyone else.'

Jake felt desperate. He knew Gite and Gabriel were just as worried as he was and that they were doing all they could, but he couldn't help wishing his step-dad was there too. Rick had so many contacts, he'd probably be able to organize a helicopter to fly in to pick up Shani and take her to a proper hospital, like he did when Shani's Uncle Morgan was hurt after a rhino pushed over his Land Rover.

'We must let my dad know,' he told Gabriel. 'So that he can tell Shani's mum.'

'You're right,' Gabriel agreed. 'We should have done that from the camp. I'll go to the compound and call him from there, then I'll bring back a stool for Shani.'

He lowered Shani to the floor but not before Jake had taken off his jacket and spread it on the ground for his injured friend to sit on. He wasn't going to let her sit on a dirty floor!

Gabriel was gone for no more than twenty minutes and when he returned he had the stool as promised. He put it down for Shani. 'Are you OK?' he asked.

'I guess so,' said Shani, settling herself on the low stool. 'Did you get through to Musabi?'

'Yes. I spoke to someone called Morgan.'

'My uncle!' Shani said, tears filling her eyes at the mention of him. She reached for Jake's hand and gripped it tightly. 'What did he say?'

'He was very, very upset at first. But when he heard you were at the hospital and that we were all with you, he felt a bit better,' said Gabriel. 'He's going to tell your mother and Rick's parents, and he sends his love and said I must tell you to be *hodari*.'

'That means brave,' Shani whispered.

'And you are,' Gite said softly.

A tall, thin man came in and stood in the queue behind them. He was carrying a tiny boy who was coughing badly. 'Gite and Gabriel,' the man said, a smile spreading across his narrow, fine-featured face.

'Hello, Marishet,' said Gite and she introduced the man and his two-year-old son, Iyasu.

Marishet lived with his wife, Alem, and two other children on a small farm up in Abuna Joseph, near the conservation team's camp.

'Marishet loves the wolves. He's our honorary assistant and he keeps an eye on the packs when he's out tending his sheep,' Gite told Jake and Shani.

The peasant farmer nodded. 'Before we met the conservation people, I used to chase the wolves from our land. I thought they would steal our sheep. But I have learnt that they prefer to eat the moles and rats,' he said. 'Now I don't chase the wolves, and I don't have a problem with rats eating my grain.'

'Do you have dogs?' Jake couldn't resist asking, and he felt Shani's grip tighten on his hand.

'Just one,' replied Marishet, then as if he understood what was behind the question, he added,

'And he's been vaccinated against rabies. That's something else we learnt from Gite and the others.'

'Just as well,' Jake said grimly.

Marishet gave Jake a puzzled look.

'There was a nasty incident this morning. That's why we're here,' Gabriel put in. He nodded to Shani. 'There was a dog attack. We think he might have had rabies.'

Marishet stared in horror at Shani then back at Celia. 'Rabies!' he gasped so loudly that others in the waiting room spun round and gawked at him. Iyasu looked at his father with wide brown eyes, then burst into tears.

'It's OK,' Marishet said, patting his son on the back. To calm the nervous looking crowd in the waiting room, he raised his other hand and added, 'No one has rabies here.' In a low voice he said to Gite and Gabriel, 'How can you be sure the dog was,' he dropped his voice further, 'rabid?'

'We won't know for certain until a sample of the brain tissue has been tested,' Gite told him.

'But from the way the dog behaved, we expect the results to come back positive,' said Gabriel.

Marishet gave Shani a sympathetic look. 'You must be in a lot of pain, and very afraid too.'

'It hurts,' Shani confessed. 'But at least I can get a vaccination. It was too late for the poor dog. And maybe even for other dogs and wolves that it bit before me.'

Her words made Jake wonder again whether there wasn't a way that the wolves could be inoculated against the terrible disease. 'Can't you vaccinate the wolves in advance, like you do dogs?' he asked Gite. 'I mean, not wait until *after* they've been bitten.'

The vet sighed, her lovely face taut with worry. 'It's difficult. We're testing oral vaccine, but the results aren't very promising at this stage.'

A nurse hurried past and Jake stepped in front of her. 'Excuse me,' he said, and the nurse had to stop short so she wouldn't collide with him. 'We need a doctor badly.'

The nurse looked very flustered. 'Everyone here needs a doctor badly,' she said and tried to brush past him.

'But you don't understand,' Jake insisted. 'It's an emergency.'

'Every case is an emergency here,' said the nurse.

'This place is overcrowded. How many doctors are on duty?' Gabriel demanded, with a sweeping gesture that took in the waiting room and all the sick people.

'Not enough,' said the nurse and hurried away.

Gite put a hand on Shani's shoulder. 'Do you think you can hold out a while longer?' she asked kindly.

Shani looked down and nodded. 'It's the same for all of us,' she said. 'We have to wait our turn.'

Their turn didn't come until the evening and by then Jake had almost given up hope that they'd be seen to that day. When a nurse finally showed them into a tiny consulting room, he could hardly believe it.

'What can I do for you?' asked the doctor, an exhausted-looking young woman whose nametag read Dr Tsehay. She smiled sympathetically when she noticed Shani hobbling in, supported between Jake and Gabriel.

'A dog bit me,' Shani explained. 'I need a rabies injection, an antibiotic, and an anti-tetanus shot.'

The doctor looked startled and Jake assumed it was because Shani seemed to know exactly what had to be done.

But he was wrong.

'Antibiotics and anti-tetanus I can do,' said the doctor. 'But not rabies vaccine. We don't have any.'

EIGHT

No rabies vaccine! The chilling announcement sent Jake reeling, and he felt Shani freeze beside him. 'You *must* have some!' he cried to the doctor.

She shook her head sadly. 'Not a single dose. I am very sorry.'

Gabriel's deep blue eyes flashed with anger. He put an arm around Shani who seemed too shocked to say anything. 'Why is there no vaccine? What kind of hospital is this?'

The doctor ran her hand wearily across her forehead. 'We usually have a good stock, but we ran out just this morning after some children were bitten by a dog. We're going to order a new batch, but there'll be a delay. It has to come from Addis, and because it's Saturday, we can't place the order until Monday morning when all the offices are open again.'

'How long will it take to get here?' Jake cut in, only vaguely aware of how abrupt and rude he sounded.

'I can't say for certain. Late Monday or some time

on Tuesday, perhaps,' said the doctor, unwinding the bandage on Shani's leg.

'But she needs the vaccine now,' Jake insisted. 'She can't wait that long.'

'Actually, that's not quite true,' Gite said. 'We can afford to wait a few days, as long as Shani has the first dose of vaccine within about seventy-two hours.'

Jake did a quick mental calculation. Seventy-two hours sounded a lot but it was only three days and nights from when Shani was bitten. She'd need the vaccine by Tuesday morning at the latest. 'What if it doesn't get here in that time?' he demanded.

No one seemed prepared to answer him so Jake came up with a solution. 'We'll have to fly back to Tanzania straight away,' he said.

The doctor was examining the wound. 'That's an option,' she agreed, looking over her shoulder at him. Her brown eyes were full of sympathy. 'But it will be difficult to get a flight at such short notice. And, really, Shani's in no state to go on such a journey. This wound is already infected.' She filled a syringe with an antibiotic and injected it into Shani's calf, right next to the bite.

Shani flinched with pain and tried to speak but was overcome by huge, heart-rending sobs.

Jake put his arms around her and held her close to him. 'Everything's going to be all right,' he promised her for the second time that day. But he knew his promise was an empty one. There was nothing he could do, and the odds seemed stacked against his friend.

The doctor gave Shani an anti-tetanus shot before putting a fresh bandage on the wound. 'You'll have to stay here for a few days so that I can keep an eye on you. With a bit of luck, the vaccine will arrive in good time and then, as long as your leg's looking good, you can be discharged.'

'Luck!' Jake said scornfully. That was the last thing he wanted to rely on. 'There must be something else we can do,' he insisted.

'What we have to do,' said Gite reluctantly, 'is tell your parents that there's been a delay with the vaccine. We'll phone again from the compound.'

Jake and Gabriel helped Shani into a wheelchair then pushed her to a small ward. There were five other patients and they were all asleep except for one, a man whose head was almost completely covered by bandages. Only his eyes, nose and mouth were visible. Jake wondered what had happened to him but knew it would be impolite to ask so he simply nodded in greeting to him.

'I haven't got any pyjamas with me,' sobbed Shani when she was sitting on the narrow bed.

'That's all right,' said the nurse. 'We'll lend you some.' She fetched a pair of blue and white striped pyjamas, then drew a curtain round the bed while Shani changed.

'I look like a prisoner,' Shani said when the nurse opened the curtain again.

'You do a bit,' smiled Jake, trying to be cheerful for Shani's sake. The pyjamas were several sizes too big for her and she looked like a tiny, scared child lying rigid under the sheet.

The medication was starting to work and Shani's eyes began to droop. 'I'm very sleepy,' she murmured.

Jake squeezed her hand. 'You'll get a vaccination before it's too late, even if I have to go and fetch it myself,' he promised quietly as she drifted away.

At the conservation team's compound a few streets away, Jake made a call to Musabi. This time, Rick answered. As soon as he knew it was Jake, he asked how Shani was.

'Sleeping,' said Jake, then he told Rick about the vaccine situation. 'We can't just wait and hope the stock will arrive before Tuesday morning. Isn't there anything you can do?'

'Like what?' Rick responded, his voice tight with worry.

'I don't know, like get a medical rescue helicopter to fly some in to us,' said Jake. 'Or at least to pick Shani up.'

'I wish I could,' said Rick. 'But I don't think the Ethiopian authorities would be happy to let someone fly into their country without going through the proper channels. It would take several days to sort things out, and we don't have that kind of time.'

Jake's heart sank. There had to be a back-up plan in case the vaccine didn't arrive on time. 'You *must* think of something,' he urged Rick, and he thought of Shani's mum and how she'd probably go mad with worry when she heard there was no vaccine. 'Don't you know anyone in this country who can help us?'

'I'll see what I can arrange,' was all Rick could promise.

A persistent ringing in Jake's head jolted him out of a strange dream. It was only when he opened his eyes and looked around the dark room that he realized the jangling noise was the phone. He leapt up from his mattress on the floor and was at the desk in two strides.

'Hello,' he said, picking up the receiver.

'Jake!' It was Rick's voice.

Please let him have good news! 'Have you sorted something out?'

'Maybe,' came Rick's reply so that Jake started to breathe a little easier. 'I thought you'd want to hear about it straight away.'

Just then, Gite came in from her bedroom. 'Who is it?' she asked, looking worried.

'My dad,' Jake told her, then, impatient to hear what Rick had sorted out, asked him, 'So what's the plan?'

'I've thought of someone in Ethiopia who might be able to help us. He's a doctor that stayed in Musabi a few years ago. He lives in a town called Gonder which is to the west of Lalibela, so I'll ring him first thing to see if he has some vaccine and can get it to you,' said Rick.

'Great!' Jake felt hopeful for the first time in hours. 'Thanks, Rick, you're a star.' After he hung up, he told Gite about the plan.

Gite was warming some milk on the stove. She put a spoon of honey in two mugs then smiled at Jake. 'You know, it'll probably be all right,' she said. 'The vaccine will surely arrive on Monday. We don't need to trouble the doctor in Gonder.'

'Oh yes we do,' Jake said stubbornly, realizing too late how curt he sounded. In a more polite tone, he added, 'I mean, it might not get here, and then Shani will be in real danger. We must have plan B, just in case things go wrong.'

'Perhaps you're right,' said Gite, pouring the milk into the mugs and giving Jake one.

Jake drank the milk then went back to bed, feeling a lot easier. *Rick always comes through when we need him*, he thought, feeling a rush of warmth for his step-dad.

There was another call from Rick soon after dawn. 'Just to let you know that Dr Fekadu is on his way with the vaccine.'

'You're the best!' was Jake's immediate reaction. He couldn't wait to tell Shani and was halfway out of the door, intending to run to the hospital, when Gabriel, awakened by the phone, came in from the bedroom.

'Going somewhere?' he asked.

'Yes. To tell Shani the good news,' said Jake and, realizing that Gabriel himself hadn't heard about it either, he quickly filled him in.

'Excellent!' said Gabriel. 'But now, can you remember how to get to the hospital?'

'Er, no,' Jake said sheepishly and waited while Gabriel put on his shoes.

Leaving Gite asleep, they hurried through the town as it was beginning to wake up. Roosters crowed behind bamboo fences and dogs yapped to one another as if they were passing a message from one end of the street to the other.

Even though it was Sunday, early traders were setting up their wares at the best spots next to the road, and one or two shoppers were already out, looking for a bargain. Further down the road, a battered taxi stopped to ask Jake and Gabriel if they needed a ride. But by then, they were just around the corner from the hospital.

Jake was surprised to see that a queue had already formed with people spilling out on to the road. 'Crumbs!' he muttered. 'Have they been there all night?'

'I don't think so,' Gabriel told him. 'But they were probably here before dawn.'

Having waited for hours with Shani last night, Jake could only sympathize with those in the queue.

Shani was sitting up in bed drinking a glass of water when they went into the ward. She looked at them expectantly. 'Back so early?' she said then flinched as she straightened her legs. The bite was obviously still hurting a lot.

'Yes, and brilliant news, Shani. My dad's got hold of a doctor who's going to bring you the vaccine. He'll be here later today.'

Shani looked as if the world had been taken off her shoulders. 'Ishee!' she said. 'That's cool. Then we'll be able to get back to helping the wolves.'

'Trust you,' chuckled Jake, but he was having similar thoughts too. Once Shani was out of hospital and her leg not hurting her so much, everything would be back on track. And now that they'd had a rabies scare themselves, they knew how horrifying it was to come into close contact with the terrible disease. Perhaps they'd even be able to persuade lots more farmers to vaccinate their dogs so that everyone would be safe.

Jake and Gabriel sat with Shani for a while, then when the nurse came to give her a painkilling injection and change the dressing on her wound, they headed back to the compound, promising to return later in the day. 'With the vaccine,' Jake said with determination.

Gite met them at the compound gate. She looked

tense. 'There's trouble,' she said as they went inside. 'Up at the camp.'

'What kind of trouble?' Gabriel asked.

'Celia has just phoned. The local people have heard about the attack on Shani. They're angry because they think they're all at risk,' Gite explained.

'Well, of course they're at risk,' Gabriel said gruffly, 'if they're not willing to have their dogs vaccinated.'

'Yeah, maybe this will persuade them once and for all that they have to get it done,' Jake chipped in.

Gite shook her head. 'You don't understand. They don't believe it was a dog that bit Shani. They think it was a wolf.'

Jake could hardly believe his ears. 'But it *was* a dog! I saw it with my own eyes. So did Celia and Mengistu.'

'That's what Celia and Bedassa told them,' said Gite. 'But the people think they're lying.'

Jake was confused. 'Why would they think that?'

Gabriel sat down and wearily ran his hands through his thick black hair. 'Word must have got round that Ras is in quarantine. Now the people are suspicious of all the wolves and expect us to do something about them.'

'That's ridiculous!' Jake declared. 'Not what you're saying,' he added quickly to Gabriel. 'What the people think. It's nonsense.'

'We know that,' said Gite. 'But the people say we're blaming the outbreak on dogs to protect the wolves.'

Jake's solution to that was easy. 'They only need to see the dog, then they'll be convinced.'

'It's too late for that,' Gite sighed. 'Bedassa burnt the body last night after Celia removed the brain tissue for the lab test.'

'Oh, no,' Jake groaned.

'We'll have to go back up to the camp,' Gabriel decided. 'Neither we nor the wolves can afford this kind of bad press. We've got to set the record straight.' He leaned out of the door and called to the sabanjia who immediately went round to where the mules were kept.

Moments later, two mules were standing in the yard, waiting for Gite and Gabriel to ride them back up to Abuna Joseph. Jake assumed he would be staying behind in Lalibela where he could be close to Shani. And also because Mengistu would want them to be together in the same place.

Jake felt a moment's frustration at missing out on the chance to do something really important to help the wolves and this made him feel a bit guilty. *Shani probably needs me more*, he told himself.

'You ready, Jake?' Gabriel's voice broke into his thoughts.

'Huh? Ready for what?'

'Aren't you coming up to the camp?'

'But I thought you and Gite . . .'

'No, I'm staying here to keep Shani company and to make sure she gets the vaccination,' Gite explained. 'It's better if you go up, Jake, because you were the first one to see the dog. Perhaps people will be more ready to believe you than one of us, especially as you're not a permanent member of the conservation team.'

Jake was more than village to go, but part of him was reluctant to leave Shani. He didn't want her to feel abandoned while he was fighting for the wolves.

But Shani wouldn't have it any other way. 'You're no good to the wolves if you're stuck here with me,' she told Jake when he and Gabriel popped in to see her on their way out of Lalibela. 'Don't forget, we came to Ethiopia to help with the wolves, not to hang around the hospital.'

Jake simply had to give her a hug. Shani was completely unselfish even though she was still in a lot of pain. She didn't deserve what had happened to her. 'I'll phone from the camp to let you know what's happening,' he promised. 'And also to find out exactly when you get the vaccine.'

'As soon as that happens, I'll be out of here like a shot,' said Shani. 'This afternoon, with any luck.'

'I hope so,' said Jake, feeling a moment's doubt. Was it really as simple as that? Perhaps Shani would have to be observed for a while to make sure she didn't get ill, rather like Ras. *But not as long*, Jake hoped.

* * *

A small group of angry people was waiting at the camp when Jake and Gabriel rode in late that afternoon, tired, hot and hungry after their day in the saddle.

The people, most of them peasant farmers, Gabriel told Jake, had been sitting on the ground but stood up the moment they saw the two riders. There was no sign of Celia and Bedassa and Jake guessed they were out monitoring the wolves and scouring the mountain for other sick-looking dogs before it got too dark.

Still sitting on his mule, Gabriel greeted the farmers politely, then told them something in Amharic.

The response was hostile. One or two people raised staffs in the air and shouted, while others shook their heads or stood with folded arms, glowering at Gabriel.

'What did you tell them?' Jake asked as he and Gabriel dismounted.

'The usual. That rabies is spread by dogs, and that the wolves could be wiped out by the disease if people don't vaccinate their dogs,' he replied. 'But they'll have none of it. They insist that the wolves are the problem.'

To Jake the situation seemed hopeless and he was filled with rage at the farmers' attitude. It was like they were blind to the real truth. He pictured Shani lying in her hospital bed waiting for the rabies vaccine and he couldn't stay quiet another second. 'It *was* a dog that bit Shani,' he insisted. 'I saw it with my own eyes. You must listen to Gabriel,' he begged.

A murmuring broke out in the crowd when those who could understand English translated what Jake had said. Everyone fell silent as a man dressed in white robes called out from the back of the group, 'If the wolves are not the problem, then why is one being kept here?' He pointed toward the enclosure where Ras was in quarantine. 'And being treated for rabies?'

Jake looked toward the quarantine pen, hoping to get a glimpse of Ras, but the bamboo fence obscured his view. 'How did they find out about Ras?' he whispered to Gabriel. 'And about Shani too?'

Gabriel shrugged. 'Someone must have seen us riding down the mountain yesterday, and Bedassa bringing Ras in the other day, then put two and two together.'

'And made four hundred,' Jake remarked grimly.

'Yes. And word spreads fast in these mountains,' said Gabriel.

The farmers demanded to know the answer to the man's question about Ras. 'Tell us why that wolf is being treated for rabies,' someone called out.

'If you do not do something about the wolves soon, we will,' said the white-robed man. 'Keep them away from us, or we will set out more poison. We cannot risk our children being attacked.'

Gabriel's eyes flashed with anger. 'A rabid wolf will probably never go near you or your children,' he explained in a voice that could have cut through steel. 'It will just get sick and die, but a dog with rabies becomes savage and attacks anything in its path.'

'Like what happened to Shani,' Jake put in.

But the people had lost patience and turned away.

'Please don't poison the wolves,' Jake shouted after them, but no one took any notice.

A feeling of complete hopelessness settled on him like a cloud. He looked up to the grassy plateau where Ethiopian Wolves had roamed freely for centuries. Could the few remaining animals survive this latest onslaught?

He had a flash back to the Zambian elephants that had been breaking out of their reserve to find food and water on the surrounding farms. The local people had also vowed to take matters into their own hands, but at least the elephants could be moved to a safer place. The wolves couldn't. *They have nowhere else to go*, Jake thought, remembering that the highlands was their only habitat, and even that was growing smaller.

A chill ran down his spine, not from the cold that was closing in with the end of the day, but from a sudden fear that the people might have started poisoning the wolves already. Were the four families of wolves in Abuna Joseph still intact?

'We must check on Etna and her pups,' he said to Gabriel as they led the mules toward the pen. 'And see how Ras is, too.'

'Celia and Bedassa will have been patrolling the wolves' ranges for most of the day,' Gabriel replied. 'They'll know if anything serious has happened. But we'll have a look at Ras just as soon as these mules are inside.' He opened the gate and slapped his mule gently on the rump to make him go into the enclosure. Shani's mule, Angel, trotted over and greeted her companion, nuzzling his neck as if she'd missed him.

Jake untacked Emperor and directed him towards the pen too. The mule refused to go in. He skittered away from Jake and went to stand on some low flat rocks. 'Stupid mule!' Jake said crossly, going after him. 'You look like a mountain goat.'

The mule lifted his head and brayed, then snorted and looked down his long nose at Jake.

'Oh, OK, then. You don't look like a goat,' said Jake. 'You're more like a . . . a . . .' He searched for a fitting term to describe the arrogant expression on the mule's face. Only one thing came to mind. 'Emperor. You're like an emperor.'

'A tyrannical one,' said Gabriel.

Emperor's comical behaviour helped to lighten Jake's mood. 'Would Your Majesty mind going in to your chambers?' he chuckled. 'Or you could stay out here and be eaten by hyenas.'

To Jake's amazement, Emperor stepped down from his rocky pedestal at once and trotted into the pen where he drank from the stone water trough before tucking into the bale of fresh hay in one corner.

'Let's go to Ras now,' said Jake, impatient to see the wolf again.

They went over to the quarantine enclosure and slipped quietly round the screen. Jake expected Ras to be hiding behind the rocks or lurking on the far side of the pen, but he was only yards away, just inside the fence. He looked magnificent. He was standing quite still, staring at the ground, his body taut and ears pricked up as if he was listening out for something.

'I think he's on to a mole,' whispered Gabriel.

Suddenly Ras pounced. In a split second, he'd caught a giant mole-rat that had popped up from below the ground.

Jake felt a little sorry for the unsuspecting creature that had instantly been turned into a wolf's dinner. 'But it shows that Ras is in good shape,' he remarked out loud, hoping that the same could be said for all the wolves in the area.

Going across to the rondavels with Gabriel a few minutes later, Jake spotted a couple of horses and their riders coming down from the plateau. It was Celia and Bedassa, returning from their day-long patrol. Jake couldn't wait to hear what they'd found and he ran to meet them.

'Is everything OK? Etna and the pups, are they safe?' he asked breathlessly.

Celia looked exhausted. 'Slow down, Jake,' she managed to smile. 'You make me feel even more worn out than I am already.' She swung one leg over the mule's back then jumped down to the ground and took off the saddle. She patted the animal on its neck and sent it into the pen behind Bedassa who was leading his horse in.

'We think the wolves are OK,' Celia continued. 'Certainly there's no evidence that any have been poisoned yet. And,' she looked at Jake, 'Etna and her pups are fine. We saw them in their den.'

'Phew,' Jake whistled in relief.

'We didn't see any others until just now when we saw Darkeena out hunting. And that's really puzzled us,' said Celia.

'Why?' Jake asked.

Gabriel had reached them and he heard what Celia said. 'Well, you know the wolves usually hunt by day,' he told Jake. 'If they're starting to become active at night, it could mean they're feeling threatened by something.'

Gabriel didn't have to spell out what that 'something' was. Jake was convinced it meant that people were already moving into the wolves' range during the day, chasing the innocent creatures and, even worse, leaving poisoned meat for them to swallow.

Remembering his promise to Shani to tell her all he could about the wolves, Jake went inside to phone her. It might help to take her mind off the bite if she heard that Etna and the pups were in good shape.

He'd made a note of the hospital's number before he left Lalibela this morning and now he took the scrap of paper out of his pocket. But before he could make the call, the phone started to ring. He picked it up.

'Jake?' came Gite's voice. Something in her tone made Jake's heart beat faster.

'Something terrible has happened,' Gite went on and Jake held his breath. 'Bandits waylaid Dr Fekadu on the way from Gonder. They stole his car.'

It took a moment for the full impact of her words to sink in. 'The vaccine!' Jake gasped.

'I'm sorry, Jake. It was taken with the car.'

NINE

Jake felt he was trapped in a never-ending nightmare. He started to speak but all that came out of his mouth was a huge sob of anguish.

Gabriel came in and took the phone from him to speak to Gite. Hearing what had happened, he hung up and rested an arm across Jake's shoulders. 'That vaccine wasn't our last hope,' he pointed out. 'There is more on the way. It's sure to get to Lalibela before long.'

'Before long?' Jake echoed, wiping his eyes with the back of his hand. 'That could mean anything. And it could be too late.'

'We must be positive,' said Gabriel.

But for Jake that was impossible. How could he feel positive when time was running out, both for Shani and the wolves?

And then, like a bell reminding everyone that nothing was on their side, the phone rang again. It was Mengistu. The results of the test on the dog's brain had just come in. They were positive.

* * *

Even before the sun was up the next morning, Jake was on his mule, riding back down the mountain to Lalibela. All he could think of now was Shani and how desperate she must be that the life-saving vaccine had been stolen. He wanted to comfort her as best he could.

He'd have gone on his own if necessary, but Celia had offered to ride with him. She could see just how desperate Jake was to be at his friend's side. 'Gabriel and Bedassa will be able to handle things up here for a few days and keep an eye out for poison in the wolves' range,' she'd told Jake. 'And Gabriel can give Ras his second vaccination.'

Before they set off, Jake went over to the quarantine pen. He wanted to see Ras one more time in case he never got to see him again.

Ras seemed to recognize Jake for he trotted over to the fence when Jake popped his head round the screen. The wolf peered expectantly at him as if he thought he might have brought him something to eat.

'Sorry, boy,' Jake said quietly. 'I've got nothing for you.' He approached the fence slowly then stopped about a metre from it, directly opposite Ras.

He expected the beautiful animal to whirl round and slink away but Ras stood still, watching Jake with narrowed, jet black eyes. Jake resisted the urge to push his hand through the fence to touch the wolf.

He's a wild animal, he reminded himself. *He shouldn't get too used to humans*.

The two kept up their mutual gaze for a while before Jake reluctantly blinked and broke the spell. 'Time to go,' he said. He took a few steps backward then turned and walked swiftly away. Just before he got to the screen he glanced back at Ras.

The wolf hadn't moved and his eyes were still locked on Jake. 'Go well,' Jake said, his words more a prayer than a farewell; with no guarantee that the vaccine would protect him from rabies, his future was unbearably uncertain. So too was Shani's. There was no guarantee that she would get her vaccine in time, and unlike with Ras, the dog that had bitten her was definitely carrying rabies.

Throughout the eight hour trek to Lalibela, Jake prayed that the stock from Addis would arrive that day. But a small voice inside kept reminding him that the order was probably only placed that morning. What chance that it would reach Lalibela the same day?

None, the voice kept telling him.

After a few hours, Celia persuaded Jake to take a rest. 'It'll make no difference if we stop for a few minutes,' she told him.

While her horse and Emperor cropped the short grass growing next to the track, and Celia sipped some water, Jake paced restlessly back and forth. His breath caught in his throat as if he was suffering from altitude sickness all over again. But he wasn't. It was sheer worry that was making him so edgy and breathless.

In the distance, he could see the tin roofs of Lalibela glinting in the sun. He looked at his watch and tried to guess how much longer it would take them to get there. *About three more hours*, he calculated. Seeing the time, he was reminded yet again that Shani had to have the vaccine before tomorrow morning if she was to be safe from the horrendous disease.

Even Rick had run out of ideas on how to help Shani. Jake had phoned him from the camp as soon as the news came in about Dr Fekadu being held up. Rick was as devastated as everyone else and while he said he'd do what he could from his end, he'd held out little hope of getting more vaccine to Shani that day.

'Then organize a flight for us to come home,' Jake insisted.

'I'll do my best,' Rick promised, saying he'd contact Jake in Lalibela the following day.

That now seemed the best option, to fly back to Tanzania where Shani was sure of getting the right medication. *We should have done that in the first place*, Jake told himself over and over again.

Impatient to be on the move, he pulled himself into the saddle and tapped Emperor on his rump. To Jake's relief, the mule responded straightaway, and that's when Jake noticed a figure waving to him from some way down the track.

Not another child begging for birr and pens, he thought irritably. Then he realized it wasn't a child coming up the hill, but a man who was also riding a mule. There was something familiar about him and when he came closer, Jake realized who it was. 'It's the man we met in the hospital queue the other night,' he said to Celia.

'Marishet?' said Celia, then, recognising him, she called down to him. 'Hello, Marishet. Are you on your way home?'

The man glanced quickly over his shoulder as if he was making sure he wasn't being followed, then kicked his mule into a trot. He'd nearly reached Jake and Celia when Jake noticed a small blue box strapped to his saddle. It looked like a cooler box.

'I think you'll be needing this,' he said, untying the box and holding it up.

Jake jumped off Emperor and hurried forward to meet him. 'What is it?'

And then, without having to open the box, he knew the answer to his question.

'Vaccine,' he breathed. 'I bet you've brought us some rabies vaccine.'

Triumphantly, Jake dashed into the ward, almost knocking over a nurse coming through the door with a tray of cups. 'It's here,' he announced at the top of his voice.

Shani was lying on her bed, staring up at the ceiling. Gite was sitting in a chair next to her, holding her hand.

The minute Shani heard Jake, she sat bolt upright. 'Vaccine?' she asked, her voice raised in hope when she saw the cooler box in his hands.

'Yep. The same lot that was in Dr Fekadu's car.'

'How –' Shani began, but Jake cut her off.

'Later,' he said. 'First you're having the vaccine.'

Celia had gone to call the doctor and now both of them came in.

'You have found the vaccine?' asked Dr Tsehay, staring at the blue box in disbelief.

'Yes. Now please inject Shani. Fast,' Jake urged, opening the box. Inside were several ampoules packed in a clear plastic container surrounded by chunks of dry ice.

Dr Tsehay smiled at Jake. 'Patience, young man. A few seconds won't make any difference, you know.'

'It could,' Jake said stubbornly. With all the bad luck going around, who knew what could happen next?

Dr Tsehay took out one of the ampoules then drew the curtain around Shani's bed. 'Maybe you'd like to wait outside in the corridor,' she said to Jake.

'OK.' Jake left the ward and stood outside by the door. Celia came with him while Gite stayed with Shani.

'Do you think it'll hurt a lot?' Jake asked Celia. Someone had once told him that the treatment for rabies was really terrible, and that a person had to have loads of shots in their stomach to be clear of the disease.

'Probably,' Celia said sympathetically. 'She'll have to have two shots to start with: anti-rabies immunoglobulin right next to the wound, then the vaccine into her shoulder muscle.'

Jake winced. But if it saved Shani's life, it was a small price to pay. 'And then what?'

'Four more injections,' Celia answered. 'One in three days' time, then four days after that, then a week later, and the last one two weeks after that.'

'Sheesh!' Jake exclaimed, using Shani's expression. 'She'll end up feeling like a pin cushion.'

A few minutes later, Dr Tsehay came out. 'You can see Shani now.'

Jake was almost reluctant to go in. He expected his friend to be in agony and was surprised to find her looking quite calm. She wrinkled her nose when he asked her how it was, but then she demanded, 'Now tell me how you found the vaccine.'

Jake told Shani, Gite and the doctor what had happened, picturing the events as Marishet had described them to him and Celia on the mountain.

Marishet was heading home after visiting his little boy who, like Shani, was still in hospital, although he was in for a bad bout of bronchitis. He took a detour to see a friend in another village and was on a road quite some way from Lalibela when he noticed three men clustered round the open bonnet of a car. They kept glancing around furtively so that Marishet grew suspicious. He knew they were up to no good and he had to find out what that no good was. He tied up his mule in some shade then went across to the men and offered his help, saying he knew something about cars.

'He didn't really,' chuckled Jake. 'He said he knows more about how a mule works. But the men were desperate enough to believe him.'

Marishet pored over the engine for a few minutes, tinkering with wires and plugs, then stood up straight and announced that a new radiator was necessary.

'He'd ridden his mule past a garage a few miles back and seen a sign that mentioned radiators,' Jake explained.

Marishet directed the men to the garage and offered to stay with the car to keep an eye on it for them. The minute their backs were turned, he opened the driver's door and looked inside. There was a black bag on the back seat, with the little blue cooler box next to it. And on the floor, behind the front seats, were three guns.

'That's when he knew the men had to be bandits,' said Jake.

Marishet looked inside the black bag and saw that

it contained doctors' instruments. And when he opened the blue box and read the labels on the ampoules, his sixth sense told him that the vaccine was meant for Shani.

He grabbed the vaccine container then leapt on to his mule and rode across the hills, eventually joining the track that led from Lalibela up to Abuna Joseph.

'And that's when he saw us,' Jake finished.

Shani had listened in wide-eyed wonder. 'Marishet's a very brave man,' she said solemnly. 'And smart.'

'What good luck that he, of all people, should have come across the bandits,' put in Gite.

'Well, it's about time we had some of that,' Jake said with feeling. 'Good luck, I mean.'

'It's also time I got out of here,' said Shani. She looked at the doctor. 'I can leave now, can't I?'

Dr Tsehay frowned. 'I don't think so. That wound's still rather serious. I'd like to keep you in another day or two.'

Shani's face crumpled. 'You can't!' she protested. 'I'm supposed to be helping out with the wolves. And I want to thank Marishet.'

'Don't worry about that,' Gite told her gently. 'Your health is much more important.'

Jake smiled to himself. He knew exactly what Shani's reaction would be.

'No, it's not,' Shani retorted. 'Sheesh! You'd think I was about to croak! I came all this way to get involved with the conservation programme. I'm not going to stay in bed because of a little bite.'

'It's not that little,' said the doctor.

'It's not that big either,' Shani insisted, and she climbed out of bed, still wearing the baggy hospital pyjamas. 'Can I have my clothes back, please?' she called to a nurse who was on the other side of the ward making notes on a patient's chart.

The nurse looked helplessly at the doctor, who, in turn, looked at Gite and Celia. 'You'll be able to keep an eye on her, but I think that will be OK, seeing as you're vets and understand about rabies.'

'Absolutely,' Celia promised. 'And we'll make sure she gets the rest of the vaccines.'

'My mum can give them to me,' Shani added. 'She's given hundreds of rabies vaccines before.' She grinned at Jake. 'Right, let's get back to the wolves!'

The first thing Shani asked when they were standing outside waiting for a taxi to take them to the compound was how Etna and her cubs were. Celia had offered to walk Emperor and her horse to the compound.

'They were fine yesterday,' Jake told her, carefully avoiding the issue of the peoples' anger and their threat to start poisoning the wolves. Shani had been through a big enough ordeal and it wasn't fair to load her with any more anxiety just yet. 'I didn't get to see them before I left, but Gabriel and Bedassa were going to ride up to them this morning. I saw Ras though and he's looking great.'

'Well, you should have checked on Etna too so that you could have told me all about the pups,' Shani scolded him with a twinkle in her dark-brown eyes. 'I could have waited an extra hour or so.'

'No you couldn't,' Jake said sternly.

Arriving at the compound, they immediately phoned Musabi to tell everyone that Shani was out of danger. Luckily, Mrs Rafiki was with Jake's parents as they'd been working on a plan to airlift Shani home.

'You can cancel that now,' Jake told Rick, and he filled him in on everything else that had happened. 'The people living near Abuna Joseph are really worried about the wolves. They think they're spreading rabies. They refuse to believe Gabriel that it's dogs that carry the disease,' he said.

'Ah, the age-old problem. People shifting the blame and not wanting to take responsibility for things,' sighed Rick. 'It happens all over the world.'

Shani spoke to her mum and promised her she'd stay out of harm's way. But the minute she hung up, she turned to the others and said, 'Right. When do we start for the camp?'

Gite and Celia must have realized there was no stopping Shani now. They exchanged a glance, then Gite shrugged and said, 'Tomorrow morning?' Looking at Jake who had flopped down on one of the mattresses, she added, 'Ready for your next mule trek?'

Jake could only nod. In truth, he was very saddle sore after four long trips between Lalibela and Abuna Joseph, but he'd never have owned up to it. And now, with Shani's crisis over, he couldn't wait to get back to the camp. The crisis for the wolves was far from over, and Jake had to do whatever he could to help them.

TEN

As soon as they arrived at the camp the next afternoon, Jake and Shani rode up to Etna's den with Gabriel.

All the way there, Jake kept looking over his shoulder, half expecting to see Mengistu tailing them even though he knew he was still miles away in Lalibela. The minder had to attend some urgent meetings about the rabies outbreak, but he'd be joining them again in a day or two. 'In the meantime, be careful,' he'd warned Jake and Shani when he stopped by the compound in Lalibela late yesterday.

On the way up to the plateau, Shani was almost beside herself with excitement. 'I kept thinking of Etna and the pups while I was lying in hospital,' she said. 'I told myself that if they were OK, I would be too.'

Not far from the spot where they always left the mules, Jake glimpsed a wolf that he thought was Darkeena darting across the plateau. He felt a surge of hope that the wolves weren't feeling threatened any more and were once again hunting by day. He wanted to mention this to Gabriel but kept it to himself, still reluctant for Shani to find out about the local farmers' hostility and their threat to set poison for the wolves.

They tethered their mules then, with Shani limping and Jake and Gabriel keeping a close watch for any suspicious-looking dogs, they made their way to the rocky shelter. Once inside, Jake looked across to the overhang.

Like the first time he'd seen the pups, it was quite shadowy in the den, so Jake waited for his eyes to adjust. But after a while, when he still couldn't see any fluffy shapes, or detect any movement, he felt his stomach churn. 'I can't see . . .' he began.

Gabriel took the words out of his mouth. 'They've gone,' said the biologist. 'The den's empty.'

Jake could hardly believe it. 'What's happened to them?' he demanded as they hurried over to the den for a closer look. There was fresh spoor all around and he hoped it wasn't hyena tracks.

Shani said nothing, her eyes welling with tears as they all stared at the empty den.

Gabriel wasn't as gloomy as Jake and Shani. 'It's a bit soon to be sure, but Etna could have moved them,' he said. 'Mother wolves often do that as a way of keeping their pups safe from predators.'

'I hope so,' Jake remarked. He didn't think he

could take any more bad news. He'd had enough to last him a lifetime.

'Perhaps we can track them?' Shani suggested as they returned to the mules.

Gabriel looked uncertain. 'You've only just come out of hospital, and you've already been on one long mule ride today. It won't be easy finding Etna, even though we know how big her pack's territory is and where the boundaries are.'

Shani wrinkled her nose but said nothing.

'Look, I know you're keen to help,' continued Gabriel. 'But don't forget you have a full day tomorrow with the school visit lined up.'

The visit was supposed to have taken place the day before but Gite had cancelled it after Shani had been bitten. Now it was on again.

'The school visits are an important part of our work,' Gabriel reminded them. 'We think you two will be able to do a great job by telling the children just how important the wolves are for Ethiopia.'

'I guess so,' Jake said unenthusiastically. He wasn't finding it easy to get worked up about going into a classroom. He'd much rather be out in the wolves' territories doing something practical like looking for newborn pups.

'I don't think you've had time to finish your preparations for the visit, have you?' Gabriel added.

'No. And that's my fault for getting bitten,' said Shani.

'Don't be daft!' Jake exclaimed. 'You couldn't help it that the dog went for you. And anyway, things have changed now. We've got a lot of new information that we wouldn't have had last week.'

Shani frowned. 'Like what?'

'Like people poisoning wolves for nothing,' Jake said without thinking. Seeing the confused look on her face, he stammered, 'Oh, of course, you don't know about that yet.'

'So tell me about it now,' Shani said firmly.

Jake filled her in on the local reaction to the news of her dog attack. 'And now they're blaming the wolves, saying they're the ones spreading rabies,' he finished.

Shani stopped dead, a look of dismay on her face. 'They can't do that,' she cried, then looking at the ground, she began to fiddle with her bead bracelet.

'What's wrong?' Jake asked worriedly, putting a hand on her arm. He thought she might be in pain again, or feeling dizzy. Perhaps she was even having some sort of reaction to the vaccine.

'This is all my fault,' she murmured.

'What is?' said Gabriel, folding his arms and looking at her.

Shani sniffed and wiped away a tear that was rolling down her cheek. 'The people being angry, their threat to poison the wolves, all of it. If I hadn't been so slow coming down that hill the other day –' she paused and glanced up to where the attack had taken place – 'that dog wouldn't have grabbed me and everything would still be fine.'

'You can't say that,' Jake tried to reason with her. 'That dog was so crazed it would have got one of us. It's just bad luck that it reached you first.'

Gabriel put his arms round Shani and hugged her. 'Now just you listen to me, young lady,' he said. 'Jake is quite right. None of this is your fault. And the poison's nothing new, it's just that people are threatening to leave more of it lying around. If anyone's to blame, it's me for not making a hundred per cent sure that you were safe. It just goes to show that no one can be prepared for what happens in the wild.'

All the way back to the camp, Jake kept his eyes peeled for the wolves. He really wanted to see Etna because then they might be able to work out where the new den was, if, indeed there was a new den. But wherever she was, she was keeping herself well hidden. So too were all the other wolves. Seeing the one darting away earlier had been a pure fluke, it seemed. The intelligent creatures must have sensed trouble after all.

They were picking their way down a steep slope when Jake noticed something stretched out on the ground some way down to his left. It looked like an animal sleeping in the fading sun, or even worse, lying dead or injured. His heart skipped a beat. 'What's that?'

Before Gabriel could reply, Jake was off his mule and running down the hill toward the animal.

'Come back!' yelled Gabriel.

But Jake didn't stop or take his eyes off the animal, searching desperately for the black and white tail, or the swollen teats that would indicate that it was Etna.

'Jake!' Gabriel called again, leaping off his mule and running after him. 'Do not go near that animal. It could have rabies.'

But Jake was already there. 'Spotted hyena!' he exclaimed, crouching next to the stiffened and bloated corpse. It hadn't been dead long, but the shape of the body showed how it had died. 'It must have been poisoned!'

Jake felt a bolt of rage for the person who'd left the poison where the animal could get it, then overwhelming pity for the hyena and the suffering it must have endured. Next, he felt enormous relief that it wasn't Etna lying there.

Shani had hobbled down to join Jake and Gabriel. She shook her head sadly and said, 'I suppose it's hard for the farmers to lose their livestock to hyenas.'

'Yeah, I know,' Jake acknowledged, thinking about the Zambian elephants again. 'But people should make a plan,' he went on. 'You can't just destroy animals because they get in your way. I mean, they have every right to be on the earth too.'

'Of course they do,' agreed Gabriel. 'But a lot of people can't see it that way, especially when their own lives are at stake. The best we can do is to protect the animals wherever we can. But we must also understand that people have needs too.' He turned to go back to the mules. 'We can't save the world, Jake. It will take everyone doing his own little bit to do that.'

Reaching their mules, they looked back. Already, a flock of vultures had landed on the dead hyena and were squabbling loudly.

And now they'll get a dose of poison as well, Jake realized. 'I know people count too,' he said miserably. 'But I wish they wouldn't do horrible things like trap animals and leave poison lying around.' As he spoke, he looked around at the vast green landscape and saw a figure moving across a nearby hillside. Jake guessed he must be a herdsman looking for stray sheep.

He was about to mount Emperor when he saw the figure on the hillside stoop down, as if he was picking something up, then he straightened up and continued on his way, only to bend down again a little further on.

'I wonder what he's doing?' he pondered aloud.

'It can only be one thing,' Gabriel said darkly. 'He's putting down poisoned bait. We'll have to pick it up.'

But Jake had already come to that decision himself. He looped Emperor's bridle around a small shrub then sprinted away across the rough stony ground to where the herdsman had left the lethal lump of meat.

By the time he got there, the man had vanished behind a ridge. Jake hunted around the hillside until he found the bait. He picked it up just as he heard Gabriel calling from a little way behind. 'There's another one here. We'll have to burn them.'

Gabriel felt in his pocket for some matches, then gathered together some dry grass and a few sticks and lit a small fire.

Relieved, Jake watched the bait turn black and shrivel up. Shani limped over and they stood in silence while the poisoned meat burned.

And then, just when he thought the immediate danger was over, Jake's eyes fell upon yet another morsel of meat, placed on top of a flat rock. 'There's loads of them!' he cried angrily.

'Yes, more than we'd expect if the people were trying to get rid of hyenas only,' said Gabriel. His eyes were grave. 'It looks like they're following through with their threat.'

Jake went to pick up the raw meat that was half-hidden in a matted clump of grass. Suddenly a furious shout rang out. 'Leave that!'

He looked up. The herdsman was striding across the hill, brandishing his crook in the air.

'No!' Jake yelled defiantly. He flung the bait on to the fire. As he did, he caught a glimpse of an animal stealing away on the far side of the hill. Its red coat and contrasting white markings were all Jake needed to identify it. 'Wolf! Over there,' he called to Gabriel.

'You're going to kill the wolves with this stuff!' he shouted to the herdsman who had broken into a run. 'And that's against the law!'

Gabriel tried to make Jake calm down. 'Careful,' he said. 'We cannot make enemies of the local people. If we do, we'll never get them to co-operate. We've got to reason with them.'

'How long will that take? And how many wolves have to die before then?' As far as Jake was concerned, talking nicely wouldn't achieve anything.

The herdsman came closer and Jake saw that he was no more than a teenager, probably only a few years older than Jake himself.

'You must not touch the bait,' the boy warned. 'We lost a sheep last night and my father is very angry. And now the wolves are biting people and giving them rabies, so we must protect ourselves.'

'Rubbish!' Shani exclaimed. 'It was a dog that bit me.'

The boy stared at her, then shook his head to show he didn't believe her, and turned to walk away.

At that moment, from high above them, came the sound of a lone wolf. '*Arooo.*' Like a warning siren, the plaintive howl rang out across the plateau.

Jake looked up, hoping to see the wolf silhouetted against the sky. But there was no sign of it.

'*Arooo.*' The cry cut through the cool afternoon air.

Was it Darkeena again? Or Etna, her sixth sense

telling her what danger the wolves faced so that now she was warning her fellows?

'You tell them,' Jake murmured. 'Tell them not to take the poison, and tell them to keep away from humans. From dogs too. You must stay safe, all of you.'

ELEVEN

'Do you think the children will take any notice of what we have to say?' Jake asked Celia on the way to the school the next morning. 'I mean, it's not as if we're teachers.'

Celia smiled. 'That's exactly why they're more likely to listen to you.'

But when they arrived on their mules at the small school that was perched on a hillside, Jake and Shani discovered that the thirty or so children gathered in the mud-walled classroom didn't want to talk about the wolves at all. The news of Shani's brush with rabies had travelled fast and the pupils were much more interested in hearing about that.

'Did the wolf just run out and bite you for nothing?' asked a girl of about ten, staring wide-eyed at the bandage on Shani's leg. Like the others, she was sitting on the floor.

'First of all, it wasn't a wolf,' said Shani. 'It was a dog.'

Jake began to feel irritated. 'It was just an unlucky coincidence,' he said.

'Did the wolf really have rabies?' said a boy.

Shani glanced at Celia who was standing at the back of the room, leaning against the wall.

'Like Shani said, it wasn't a wolf. It was a dog. And yes, it did have rabies,' said Celia.

'And I'm fine,' Shani put in hastily. 'I had a vaccination.'

Jake seized his chance. 'Just like all your dogs should have. If everyone vaccinated their dogs against rabies, there wouldn't be a problem and the wolves would be safe.' He unrolled a poster Gite had given him. It showed a rabid dog and gave information about how people could prevent this happening to their pets.

Celia gave him a thumbs up to show her approval, but the children were hardly listening. They seemed much more interested in Shani's ordeal.

'Will we have to have vaccinations too?' piped up a different girl. 'Like for yellow fever and cholera?'

'Only if you live where there are lots of animals with rabies, or . . .' Shani hesitated, obviously reluctant to go on.

'Or what?' prompted the girl.

'Or . . .' Shani sighed then said quietly, 'or if you get bitten like I was.'

It seemed they couldn't avoid the subject.

'It's better to vaccinate your dogs though.' Jake

tried to change the topic. 'Now, let's talk about the wolves. You know, you're really lucky to live in the only country on the planet where Ethiopian Wolves are found.'

'And the pups are so cute,' said Shani, and she told the pupils about Etna and her litter. 'It would be so sad if they ended up being poisoned,' she added, holding up a photograph of a litter of pups.

One of the boys put up his hand. 'My father said the wolves are a pest just like the hyenas and jackals that take our sheep. That's why we have to put down poison. And now we must get rid of the wolves because of the rabies.'

Jake bristled with anger. 'You don't have to get rid of them. Just vaccinate your dogs, that's all.' How many more times would he have to say it to get the message across?

But the boy was adamant. 'My father says the wolves are very bad news.'

'It's hopeless!' Jake said in exasperation when they came out from the school. 'It's like the children's minds have been poisoned by their parents.'

Shani agreed. 'There's too much poison going around altogether.'

Celia was disheartened too. 'I really thought we were getting somewhere with the people round here,' she sighed as they untied their mules. 'But it looks like we're back to square one.'

They trailed back into camp at the same time that

Gite and Gabriel returned from a village on the far side of the plateau where they'd been holding a vaccination clinic.

They both looked tried and frustrated. 'Only five people bothered to bring their dogs to us,' said Gite. 'We told them to spread the news about how rabies could end up costing everyone a lot if their cows and other livestock became infected.'

'Did that work?' Jake asked.

'A bit. A few more people went to fetch their dogs, but others said they thought it was a wolf problem more than anything else.' Gabriel took a wad of cards out of his shirt pocket and dumped them on the small table inside the rondavel. 'Unused vaccination certificates,' he said crossly. 'We thought we'd use up every one of them today.'

While Gite prepared supper, Jake and Shani went with Gabriel to check on Ras and to take the wolf some meat.

'We haven't had time to catch rats for him today,' Gabriel confessed. 'And I'm not sure if he's managed to get any himself in the pen, so we'll offer him the meat and see if he's interested.'

Ras was standing calmly behind the bamboo, watching them.

Jake pushed the bite-sized chunks of meat through the fence. 'Here, Ras,' he said. Looking into the wolf's intelligent eyes, he added softly, 'You know, even if you don't think so, you're pretty well off in here at the moment. People are out to get the others. At least we can keep an eye on you here and make sure you're safe.'

Ras cocked his head while Jake spoke, then half-turned and gazed out toward the mountains as if he'd understood what Jake had said and was wondering about the rest of his pack.

Jake backed away and stood with Shani and Gabriel, waiting to see if the wolf would eat.

It was a few minutes before Ras went to inspect the food. He sniffed it and licked it once or twice then suddenly froze, his eyes fixed on the ground at his feet.

Now what? Jake wondered. He just glimpsed a slight movement in the grass before Ras pounced on a mole that had scrabbled up through the soil. Holding his prey firmly in his jaws, the wolf looked at Jake as if to say, *This is what I'd rather eat, thank you very much*, before trotting to the other side of his enclosure to eat his meal in peace.

'That was amazing,' Shani breathed, her eyes as round as saucers.

Jake was glad to see for himself that wolves really did prefer freshly-caught prey. Not chunks of long-dead meat. 'Maybe they won't be so ready to take the bait that's left out for them,' he said.

Gabriel wasn't convinced. 'If a wolf's hungry and he finds meat, he'll eat it.'

They left Ras and went back to the rondavels. The

shadows were growing longer, signalling the end of the day, and Jake felt the chill of early evening biting into him. He went inside to fetch a jacket, then joined Gabriel who was building a fire outside to heat a big pot of water.

Shani stayed inside to help Gite and Celia prepare for another vaccination clinic the next day. There were pamphlets and certificates to pack as well as dozens of clean syringes and batches of vaccine.

Jake put some logs on the fire then stood up and looked down the mountain. 'Who's that?' he asked, seeing a horse and its rider coming up the track to the camp.

'It must be Bedassa,' said Gabriel. 'He's been mending predator-proof fences today. It looks like he's in a hurry. Wanting his supper, I bet!'

'He's got someone with him,' Jake remarked, seeing a smaller figure sitting in front of Bedassa.

'That's odd,' said Gabriel. 'Who's he bringing up to the camp at this time of the day?'

'A young boy by the look of it,' Jake said.

Bedassa rode up to them and swung himself off the horse while it was still trotting. Jake and Gabriel ran forward to help the boy down.

And that's when Jake noticed the huge, bleeding gash on the back of the child's arm, just above his elbow. 'Oh no! Has he been bitten?'

Bedassa nodded. 'By a wolf, he says.'

The words were like a stab to Jake's heart. He felt

sick as they took the boy inside where Gite tended to his wound. It was bad enough that the child had been bitten, but to think a wolf had done it! *That's all we need now*, Jake thought and felt a pang of guilt that for a moment he was more worried for the wolves' sake than the boy's.

The child howled in agony as Gite examined the wound. Shani tried to comfort him, putting her arms around him and telling him he'd be fine.

'I was bitten too,' she told him and showed him the bandage on her leg. 'But I'm OK now.'

'I know. I saw you today,' sobbed the child, and that's when Jake recognized him.

'You were at the school,' he said. It was the boy who'd been so hostile about the wolves, repeating his father's words about the animals being bad news.

It seemed that the man had been proved right. Did this mean the rabies had definitely spread to the community of wolves?

Jake felt thoroughly depressed. Once again, he half-wished he was at home in Musabi and had never heard of the Ethiopian Wolves. At least that way he'd have been spared the heartache of seeing them dying around him.

Gabriel crouched down in front of the child. 'What's your name?'

'Joseph,' sniffed the boy.

'Where do you live, Joseph?'

The boy described where his home was. 'My brother has gone to tell my father,' he said.

'Tell us what happened,' Gite prompted.

'My brother and I were looking for a sheep inside a cave. A wolf jumped out at me and grabbed my arm and bit it,' sobbed Joseph.

'Are you sure it was a wolf?' Jake asked.

'Yes. I saw its white legs,' said Joseph, tears coursing down his cheeks. 'And its black tail when it was running away.'

Jake's heart sank even more.

Bedassa came in and picked up the story. 'I was riding past the cave and heard a scream. I caught a glimpse of an animal dashing away . . .'

'What did it look like?' Jake had to know.

'I didn't get a good look,' Bedassa confessed. 'I only saw its tail as it disappeared round the side of the cave. But it could have been a wolf.' His tone was grim.

Celia had been to fetch a bowl of warm water from the pot on the fire outside. She put it on the ground next to Joseph and poured in some disinfectant before gently bathing the boy's arm. The bite was very bad, worse than Shani's had been.

'We'll need to get him to hospital as soon as possible for proper treatment,' said Gite, taking some ointment out of a first-aid box.

Joseph's eyes grew wide. 'H . . . h . . . hospital?' he stammered. 'Am I going to get rabies?'

'No,' said Shani with determination. 'You're going to have a vaccination like I did. You can have one of mine.' She fetched the blue cooler box and took out one of the ampoules. 'You can give it to him, can't you?' she asked Gite.

'Yes, but you know he can wait until we get him to hospital. The supply from Addis should have reached Lalibela by now,' said Gite. 'We don't need to use yours.'

'But what if something's gone wrong and the vaccine hasn't arrived?' Shani pressed the ampoule into Gite's hand. 'Please give it to him. It's frightening to know you've got rabies germs inside your body and there's nothing to fight them off.' She spoke rapidly, her eyes wide with panic, and Jake knew at once just how frightened she must have been when she'd heard there was no vaccine.

'You're probably right,' said Gite and she took a clean syringe out of the first-aid kit and filled it with the vaccine.

Joseph howled even louder when the needle went in and Jake had to turn away. Shani sat next to the boy, comforting him until he stopped crying. 'See? It wasn't so bad, was it?' she said, although her own eyes were filled with tears too.

The boy's father and older brother arrived on horseback half an hour later. Jake was the first to hear the horses' hooves clattering over the hard ground and he went outside with Gabriel to watch the pair galloping down a ridge west of the camp. The sun had long gone down, leaving only a smudge of light in the western sky so that the two horsemen appeared as silhouettes first of all.

'Where's my son?' demanded one of the men when they pulled up in front of the rondavels. He was wearing a thick black cloak to keep out the cold.

'It's all right, he's sleeping,' said Gabriel who was standing at the doorway with Jake.

'He must wake up. We have to take him to hospital,' said Joseph's father. He leapt down from his horse and, leaving his older son with the horses, tried to push past Gabriel.

'You can't. Not in the dark,' reasoned Gabriel.

'And you don't have to anyway,' Jake added. 'Joseph's had his first dose of vaccine.'

The father stopped and turned to look at him. 'He has?'

'Yes. Shani let him have one of hers,' he explained. 'And I think that means you've got three days before he has to have his next dose. Isn't that right?' he asked Gite, who was sitting inside the lamp-lit rondavel checking the e-mail on her lap-top computer.

'That's right,' she confirmed. 'And we've cleaned the wound and applied antibiotic cream. He'll be all right now until we can get him to hospital. I suggest you and your other son spend the night here then take Joseph down to Lalibela in the morning.'

The father looked very relieved, especially when he knelt down next to Joseph who was curled up in a sleeping bag in front of a glowing brazier. He touched the boy's forehead and whispered something. Jake thought it sounded like a prayer.

But the man's tenderness was reserved for his son alone. His anger was bubbling just below the surface when he stood up again. 'I am grateful to you all, but you must now see that we are living amongst dangerous creatures. The people are very afraid. We know of three wolves that have rabies, so there will be others. The disease is spreading like a forest fire. How long before the next child is bitten?'

'Three wolves with rabies?' Jake burst out. 'That's not true!'

'Yes, how did you come up with that number?' Gabriel queried.

Joseph stirred and his father lowered his voice. 'There's the wolf in the pen here, the one that bit Joseph, and the one that bit –' he glanced at Shani who was sitting on a stool next to a paraffin lamp. She'd been writing in her diary but now her attention was fixed on Joseph's father. 'That young lady,' the man finished.

'That was no wolf!' Shani exclaimed. She stood up and put her hands on her hips, resting her weight on her uninjured leg. 'That was a dog. And I know a dog when I see one.' She sounded so indignant that

Joseph's father simply shrugged and said, 'If you say so.'

'And Ras hasn't got rabies,' said Jake. 'He was treated for it just in case a rabid dog bit him.'

'Or a rabid wolf,' said the man. 'And now we know for sure that it was a wolf that attacked Joseph.'

Jake couldn't argue with him. He had no proof himself, one way or the other. But from Joseph's description, the animal certainly sounded like a wolf.

Celia came in carrying a tray of mugs and a pot of steaming coffee. Behind her was the man's other son and as he came into the softly lit rondavel, Jake recognized him. 'You're the one who was spreading bait around the wolves' range yesterday!'

'And now you see why we must do it.' The teenager looked at his sleeping brother then back at Jake. 'If you hadn't picked up the bait yesterday, that wolf might never have bitten Joseph,' he said accusingly.

Jake felt utterly helpless. There was nothing he could say to stand up for the wolves now.

Gabriel tried to buy some time. 'Please don't take matters into your own hands just yet,' he appealed to the father. 'We're monitoring the wolves very closely and haven't seen any with rabies yet. But I give you my word, I will go out first thing in the morning and look for the animal that bit Joseph.'

'I'll help you,' Jake volunteered. He stared out of the door toward the looming bulk of Abuna Joseph, thinking of the four packs of wolves hidden by the darkness and the mist – the River family, the Cliff group, the Ridge pack and Etna's family, the Plateau pack. *What's happened to Etna and her pups?* he wondered for the thousandth time. For Jake, the little family had come to represent all the Ethiopian Wolves. The four pups symbolized hope for the future of the precious creatures, but their sudden disappearance showed how they could be on the verge of vanishing off the face of the earth altogether.

Just then, from the direction of the quarantine pen, came the eery howl of a single wolf. *Arooo*.

'Ras!' Jake breathed.

Ras howled again, a lonely cry that resonated in the darkness.

What if rabies wipes out all the wolves here? Jake thought desperately. *Ras could end up being the only one left.*

TWELVE

Jake and Gabriel figured that the best starting point in their search would be the cave where Joseph was attacked. Gabriel knew where it was, a good hour's ride from the camp, so he and Jake set off at dawn, riding in the opposite direction to the father and his two sons who had already mounted their horses and headed down the track to Lalibela.

Shani ached to join Jake and Gabriel but her good sense told her she'd only hold them up.

'It's too dangerous for you,' Jake told her protectively. If there was a rabid animal out there, Jake wasn't going to allow Shani to go anywhere near it.

The cave was just outside the wolves' range in a valley that lay between two ridges. Jake and Gabriel dismounted and tethered their mules to a tree before walking over to the cave.

'Keep your eyes wide open,' Gabriel warned.

Jake hardly needed to be told. He certainly didn't intend for his name to be added to the list of those that he knew had been bitten. *First Ras, then Shani, then Joseph. There'll be no more*, he thought grimly.

Near the mouth of the narrow cave, they came across the body of yet another dead animal, this time a golden jackal.

'Poisoned,' Gabriel reported, looking down at the undamaged sand-coloured coat.

'That's two poisoned animals I've seen now,' Jake said gloomily. 'Who knows how many others there are?' His fear for Etna and her pups grew bigger. Was the empty den really a sign that Etna had moved her little family, or did it point to something a lot more sinister?

There were scuff marks in a patch of soft ground at the entrance to the cave. 'This is probably where Joseph was attacked,' said Jake, bending down for a closer look.

Gabriel was about twenty metres away, looking around for other marks, such as tracks that might show them the direction the animal had taken. 'Not a lot to go by here,' he said, examining a tuft of hair caught in a bush. 'This is sheep's wool.'

Jake peered into the dark cave. 'Maybe the wolf's inside, like it was when Joseph was bitten. I'll have a look, shall I?' he called over his shoulder to Gabriel

'Not alone,' ordered Gabriel. 'I'll come with you. Hold on a second. What's this?'

Jake turned to see Gabriel picking something up.

'More bait,' said the biologist. 'And it's fresh. We're

not the only ones looking for the animal that bit Joseph.' He pulled a face. 'Not that a rabid animal will eat anything. Very often they can't swallow, and sometimes their jaws are paralysed.'

With a heavy heart, Jake turned to go into the cave and as he did, he heard a strange, gurgling sound coming from the gloomy interior. 'What . . .' he began, then gasped when he saw something hurtling towards him. He caught a glimpse of steely grey eyes, flashing teeth and a long narrow face twisted with rage before he spun round and ran blindly forward.

He was vaguely conscious of Gabriel staring at him in horror and of a savage snarl coming closer, so close that Jake was sure he could feel the creature breathing down his neck. He ran on, expecting to feel a powerful jaw clamping round his leg at any moment.

'Help!' he screamed. But the only thing that could stop the crazed animal was a gun, and Gabriel was not armed. The bite would come at any time and Jake's name would be added to the list of those who'd stared the rabies curse in the face.

So gripped by fear was Jake that it took a few seconds before he realized that Gabriel was calling out to him.

'It's OK,' he said. 'You're safe now.'

Jake spun round. Nothing was chasing him. He looked back at Gabriel in confusion. 'But that's impossible. There was a crazed animal right behind me. I saw it.'

'Over there,' said Gabriel, pointing towards the cave.

Jake turned round again and saw what had happened. Lying on the ground, partly hidden by a bush and with its head caught in a noose, was a scrawny black and white dog. It wasn't moving and Jake knew it was dead, strangled by the loop of rope.

He started to tremble when he realized what a narrow escape he'd had. But deep inside he also felt pity for the wretched creature whose protruding ribs and hipbones showed it hadn't eaten in ages.

Gabriel came over and put his hand on Jake's shoulder. 'That was close,' he said.

Jake could only nod. Where had the noose come from? he wondered. He followed the rope with his eyes. It was dangling down from a ledge just above the cave and when Jake saw that someone was holding the end, he gasped with surprise.

'Marishet! It's you!' He was too astonished to ask how Marishet had been in the right place at the right time – again.

Marishet let go of the rope so that it fell to the ground and coiled round the dog like a snake. Then he climbed down from the ledge with an agility that told Jake the man was more at home in the mountains than anywhere else. *Like the wolves*, he thought fleetingly.

Marishet came to stand with Jake and Gabriel. Jake noticed he was carrying a small box, rather like the cooler box that had contained Shani's vaccine.

'I was out looking for bait for I have heard about the poison threats,' Marishet explained, opening the box. Inside were a few pieces of dirt-encrusted meat. 'I was up there,' he pointed to the area above the cave, 'when I saw you two tying up your mules so I came to meet you. When I got to the ledge, I heard you screaming, Jake, then saw the dog chasing you. Luckily I had a rope so I was able to use it like a lasso.'

Jake was astounded that Marishet's aim had been so accurate and his reflexes so sharp. 'Thank you, Marishet. You saved my life.'

'Now that's probably an exaggeration.' The man smiled modestly.

'We don't know that,' said Jake. 'But one thing's sure. You're brilliant at arriving on the scene when we need you.'

'Like a guardian angel,' grinned Gabriel.

Marishet shook his head. 'No, I'm just watchful. Like the conservation team have asked me to be. I could tell immediately that the dog was out of its mind, poor thing.'

Jake knew at once that this dog was the same animal that had bitten the young boy. 'Joseph only *thought* he saw a wolf,' he said, 'because of the white legs, and because it's dark inside the cave.'

'And because he saw what he expected to see,' Gabriel added. 'Not what was really there.'

They buried the dog in a shallow grave that they scraped out of the ground using flat stones, then walked back to the mules. Bedassa would have to return later in the day for the body so that the usual brain tests could be carried out.

Jake felt more hopeful than he had in days. 'At least we know for sure that it's dogs that are the problem, not the wolves.'

'*We* do. And we've always known that,' Gabriel reminded him. 'But we still have to convince the people so that they stop persecuting the wolves and take their dogs to be vaccinated.'

'Leave that to me,' said Marishet. 'I have an idea. But first, I must check on something.'

He would give no more details, or even an inkling of what he had in mind, and, with a cheery wave, strode off towards a settlement on a hill beyond the cave.

All the way back to the camp, Jake kept hoping to see a wolf. He especially wanted to see Etna again. 'Can we check her den to see if she's gone back there?' he asked Gabriel when they were passing a few hundred metres in front of the rocky overhang.

'Sure,' said Gabriel.

But the den was still empty and, going right up to it, Jake and Gabriel didn't see any fresh droppings or spoor that might show the wolves had been there recently. It was like an old house that had long been abandoned.

'What's happened to them?' Jake asked with a mixture of frustration and anxiety. 'If Etna did move the pups to another den, surely someone would have seen them by now?'

Gabriel shrugged. 'We just have to hope for the best,' was all he could say.

THIRTEEN

Jake and Shani spent the rest of the day observing Ras from behind the bamboo screen, and watching for wolves from the hill behind the camp.

'He seems restless today,' Jake said, observing Ras pace up and down inside the fence.

'Poor boy,' said Shani. 'It must be like being stuck in hospital even though you feel fine. I was lucky to be there for such a short time, with people I could talk to.'

'And we're not much good as companions to Ras,' Jake pointed out. The wolf was definitely getting used to the humans, but judging from his lonely cry last night he longed to be with his own kind.

'I wonder how Joseph is?' said Shani.

Jake glanced at his watch. 'He's probably just arriving at the hospital.' It was at least eight hours since the boy had left the camp with his dad and brother.

'Just think, you could have been on your way there

now as well,' Shani remarked. 'If Marishet hadn't turned up with that rope.'

Jake grimaced. 'I'd have refused to go. You'd have given me some of your vaccine too, wouldn't you?'

'Maybe,' Shani teased.

Ras was standing quietly at the fence, staring out with a look of longing on his intelligent face. He pricked up his pointed ears, listening to sounds that Jake and Shani couldn't hear.

'Perhaps he's heard another wolf?' Shani suggested.

Jake held his breath, hoping to hear something too. 'Nothing,' he said after a while. Abuna Joseph was eerily quiet, like a sleeping house in the dead of night.

But then, above the silence, came the faint sound of people talking. Jake looked back at the rondavels, hoping that another group of farmers hadn't arrived to insist something be done about the wolves. But the only person he saw was Bedassa, stoking the fire where he would soon burn the dog's body.

'That's funny,' said Jake. He realized the voices were coming from higher up the mountain. 'Let's go and see,' he said to Shani.

Not knowing what to expect, they left Ras and started up the hill behind the rondavels. The voices grew louder but they didn't sound angry. Instead, the sound was like a busy market, with dozens of people all talking at once.

Cresting a hill, Jake and Shani saw what was

making all the noise. Only it wasn't a crowd of humans.

'Baboons!' exclaimed Shani. 'Hundreds of them.'

Jake had never seen such a large troop. They were sunning themselves and foraging on a rocky plateau about a hundred metres away.

'They must be the Geladas, the bleeding-heart baboons Celia and Mengistu told us about,' Shani remembered.

Obligingly, one of the primates stood up and faced Jake and Shani, revealing the heart-shaped patch of red skin on its chest.

'Thanks for introducing yourself,' Jake chuckled.

Hearing him, the big baboon bared his teeth then turned his back on Jake and Shani as if to show he wasn't in the least impressed by them, and ambled further away from the human intruders.

The two friends watched the baboons for a while before starting back down to the camp. They were almost at Ras's enclosure when they heard the mournful howl of a wolf coming from nearby.

Jake's heart leapt. Apart from Ras, it was the first wolf he'd heard in days. He looked around, hoping to see it. But the creature was as invisible as the air.

Perhaps that's how you should stay for a while, he thought. *Until the mountains are safe for you again.*

The next morning, Jake and Shani had just taken some meat to Ras when Marishet appeared at the camp. He looked pleased, as if he had some good news.

'Any luck?' Jake asked eagerly.

'Oh, yes,' smiled Marishet. 'I have arranged for a gathering on my land this afternoon. We're to have a feast for it is one of our religious festivals today, and we would like all of you to come too. Would you?'

'Sure,' said Celia, while Gite and Gabriel looked up from the lap-top and nodded.

Jake felt a little disappointed. He'd expected Marishet to announce that people had realized the wolves were not to blame for the rabies epidemic and that they'd all make sure their dogs were vaccinated against the disease. But Marishet didn't even mention rabies, other than suggesting casually that Gite brought a vaccination kit with her in case they met some dogs on the way.

'Fat lot of good that'll do us,' Jake complained when Marishet had gone. 'I mean, joining in a feast with people who aren't interested in the wolves.'

'I'm not so sure,' said Gite. 'It will give us a chance to speak to the people on friendly terms. You never know what we might achieve that way.' She looked at her watch. 'I think there's just time for me to take some blood from Ras and check for rabies antibodies,' she said.

Not knowing whether he wanted to hear the results of the test or not, Jake went with Shani and Gite to the quarantine pen. Ras was quite calm when he saw them coming so it was easy for Gite to sedate him by using a syringe attached to the end of a long pole.

Once the wolf was lying on the ground, Gite went into the pen and quickly took some blood. Then they left the wolf to sleep off the drug and went back to the rondavel. Everyone clustered around while Celia put a drop of blood on a slide to examine it under the microscope.

Jake held his breath. Next to him, Shani fidgeted nervously with her bead bracelet.

When Gite looked up, her face was so grave that Jake's heart dropped. The news was going to be bad.

'Well,' said Gite. 'The count is high.'

'Does that mean –' Shani began.

'Uh-huh,' said Gite, and now she smiled broadly. 'The anti-body titres are higher than the minimum. I think he's going to be OK.'

The news was one of the best presents Jake had ever had. He turned and hugged Shani and she cheered happily in his ear. 'I'm not the only one who's safe now,' she laughed.

The journey to Marishet's home took about an hour and a half by mule. Bedassa had volunteered to stay behind to keep an eye on Ras, so Jake and the others set off at midday.

Mengistu, the minder from the Ministry of Agriculture, had returned soon after Marishet's visit and was coming to the feast as well. He rode alongside Jake, his aristocratic black horse dwarfing Emperor.

'I bet the Australian tourist hasn't done anything like the mileage we have on the back of a mule,' Jake remarked to Shani. 'And we didn't even come to Ethiopia to go mule trekking!'

In his mind he ran through everything that had happened in the few days he and Shani had been in the country. They'd seen the most threatened canids in the world, been confronted with the harsh reality of rabid dogs and people being bitten, made desperate journeys to hospital on mules, fallen into despair over the stolen vaccine, discovered they had a guardian angel in the form of Marishet, helped out with a quarantined wolf and learnt he was going to be OK . . . The list was growing all the time. The awards committee probably never dreamed Jake and Shani would be caught up in so much drama!

Jake himself could hardly believe how much they'd experienced. But in just a few days, they'd board the plane for Tanzania, and home. *We can't go back yet*, he thought. *Not until we know the people have changed their minds about the wolves.*

From a distance, Marishet's home seemed deserted.

Gabriel frowned. 'He did say this afternoon, didn't he?'

Gite nodded.

'Maybe we're a little early,' Celia suggested.

Nearing the stone house, Jake saw a white-robed figure coming out of the door. It was Marishet, who waved to them in welcome. His wife, Alem, and his children came out to stand beside him and they nodded shyly to the visitors when Marishet introduced them.

'Come inside everyone,' beamed Marishet. 'Alem has made coffee.'

At the mention of the word, Jake a wave of nausea. 'Er, is it OK if I just have some water?'

'You can have a Coke,' said Gite who had brought some cans with her. 'I know coffee's not your favourite.'

'Thanks,' Jake said, relieved.

There was a delicious aroma inside the house.

'The food smells good,' said Celia.

'Yes, we have injera, shiro and messer,' said Marishet, then he pointed to a huge jug on a table, 'and tej.'

'What's tej?' asked Shani.

'Honey mead,' said Marishet. 'For our celebration later. But it's only for adults, I'm afraid.'

Jake was beginning to feel rather frustrated. Marishet had promised to arrange something that would help the wolves, but all he could talk about was festivals and food. It was like everyone had suddenly forgotten about the rabies problem and the threat of poisoning. And Gabriel and the others were sitting round casually drinking coffee as if they didn't have a care in the world, either.

He heard a dog yap outside and went to the door. Leaning against the jamb, he looked out, and his eyes nearly fell out of his head.

'Dogs!' he gasped. 'Dozens of them! Shani, come and see!'

A long procession of people was approaching the house, all of them with dogs trotting at their heels. There were small puppies and full-grown adults, most of them rangy animals, their colouring as varied as the landscape of Ethiopia. They barked and bounded along happily next to their owners as if they were taking part in a dog show or going out for a walk.

But Jake knew beyond a shadow of doubt that something a lot more important was going on.

'They're coming to be vaccinated!' he declared, spinning round and catching Marishet's eye. 'You *are* a guardian angel! How did you persuade everyone to come?'

'It wasn't just me,' said Marishet. 'Joseph's father, Haile, helped too.'

'Joseph's father!' Jake thought he had to be dreaming. That was the last person he expected to co-operate. When he looked out again, he saw Haile in front of all the others, carrying a black and white puppy in his arms.

Marishet finished his coffee. 'Come on,' he said,

standing up. 'We have a lot of work to do before the feast.'

Outside, they quickly set up a makeshift clinic. Jake helped Marishet carry a big home-made wooden table to a flat area in front of the house, then went back for a chair. Meanwhile, Shani and Gite took syringes and ampoules of vaccine out of the kit Gite had brought along and lined them up on the table.

'Just as well we got this ready the other day,' said Shani. 'And that we packed so many doses.'

'I always think it's better to take too much vaccine than too little,' said Gite.

'If there's any at all!' Shani quipped, catching Jake's eye.

'That's a sick joke,' said Jake, shaking his head. He picked up the vaccination certificates that had fallen off the table and arranged them into a neat stack, ready to be filled in with the dogs' details, the date and the vaccine batch number.

Gabriel, Marishet and Mengistu were organizing the people into two queues while Celia was examining each dog to make sure they were all in good health.

'We shouldn't vaccinate dogs that aren't well,' Gite explained, taking out her stethoscope to go and help Celia.

'What will you do if some are sick?' Jake asked.

'Treat them if we can and get the owner to promise to bring them back for their rabies inoculation when they're well.'

'What if they don't?' Jake persisted.

Gite looked at the people waiting patiently in the two queues. 'I think they will,' she said. 'We've never had a turn out like this before. Something's happened that made them think seriously about rabies.'

'I suppose Marishet will get round to telling us what that something was,' said Shani as Gite and Celia began to vaccinate the dogs. She and Jake sat at the table, filling in a certificate for each dog.

In the end, it wasn't Marishet who did the explaining, but Joseph's father, Haile. When all the dogs – forty-five in total – had been vaccinated and were sleeping in the shade of Marishet's house, he stood up and called for everyone's attention.

'Before we eat, I want to say a few things.' He looked at Shani and beckoned her to come over to him.

'Me?' Shani mouthed in surprise.

Haile nodded. 'First of all, I want to thank this young lady for the vaccine that saved Joseph's life.'

A ripple of excitement ran through the crowd.

'You see, the hospital in Lalibela only received its order of vaccine late today,' Haile went on. 'If we'd had to wait all this time for the first injection, I think we'd have been nearly mad with worry. But we were spared that because Shani was so generous.'

Jake was sure that under her dark skin, Shani was blushing. She started to protest. 'It was nothing . . .'

'It was everything,' declared the man. 'But we have

others to thank.' He called Gite and Celia forward. 'You all know that these ladies are vets,' he said. 'But they had the skill of doctors when they cleaned Joseph's wound. Thanks to them, the bite did not become infected and Joseph will be out of hospital in the morning.'

Haile beckoned to Jake and Gabriel. 'Here are two other heroes,' he declared. 'They went to hunt down the animal that attacked Joseph. We were sure it was a wolf, but we were wrong. It was a dog, and it almost bit Jake too.'

There were a few gasps of sympathy, then the crowd fell silent as Joseph's father raised his hands. 'We must not forget Mengistu,' he gestured towards Jake and Shani's minder who was standing next to the table, 'who shot the first dog, the one that bit Shani, and Marishet who dealt with the second dog before it could bite Jake. To make sure other dogs don't become a threat, you have brought all yours here today to have them inoculated. So we must thank you, too.'

Jake was still confused. Haile's message wasn't all that different from what the conservation team had been saying for ages – that unvaccinated domestic dogs were the problem, not the wolves.

Marishet must have noticed Jake's puzzled expression. 'There's more,' he whispered as Haile called for silence again.

'We have thanked everyone, but now there is an

apology to make. And I am the one who must make it.' He turned to Jake and the others. 'My older son and I are responsible for much. We placed poison around the mountains, we blamed the wolves when they were innocent, we refused to believe you when you told us the truth, and we encouraged people to act against the wolves. And we paid for that,' he finished quietly.

'I don't think you should blame yourself that Joseph was bitten,' said Gite. 'It was an accident.'

'No, you don't understand. We brought it on ourselves,' Haile insisted. 'You see, that black and white dog that bit Joseph was . . .' he paused, 'ours.'

Jake stared at him in disbelief. Beside him, Shani gasped.

The man went on. 'He'd been missing for ten days and we'd looked everywhere for him. It was Marishet who recognized him and took me to see the body.' He swallowed. 'We were very fond of that dog and if we had taken your advice and vaccinated him, we'd still have him today and we wouldn't have known the fear of seeing our child savaged by a rabid dog.' He looked back at the crowd. 'And that is why I have urged you all to listen to the conservation people. They are not here only for the wolves, but for us all.'

Mengistu spoke up, his deep voice carrying over the people's heads. 'The wolves are part of our mountain country just as much as we are. If we lose the wolves, we lose a part of our souls.' He met Jake's eyes and nodded, as if he finally agreed that their visit had been worthwhile.

The celebration that followed was a fitting end to a day that had seen Ras given a clean bill of health and a promise from the local people that the wolves would not be persecuted. Jake and Shani helped Marishet's wife to set the food out on the wooden table, then the people formed a queue and helped themselves.

When everyone had feasted, and the dogs had been given the leftovers, Mengistu fetched his guitar. 'Now the party really starts,' he said.

A few people stood up and began to dance, shyly at first, then, as others joined in, they abandoned themselves to the rhythm of the music. It was as if everyone's worries had been washed away and when Jake saw two young dogs playing together as if they were dancing too, he found himself laughing out loud for the first time in days.

But it was only on the way back to the mountain camp that his day was made complete. He'd been riding a little way behind the others, lost in his thoughts, when he felt as if something was staring at him. He stopped Emperor and looked behind him, right into the eyes of a wolf.

The magnificent creature was standing on a rock not far away, silhouetted by the setting sun. It was watching Jake, not in fear, but with a look of intense interest.

What is it? Jake asked silently.

As if in answer, the wolf glanced to one side. Jake followed the animal's gaze and his heart leapt. In a hollow in the ground were four little wolves, tumbling together in play.

'Etna!' Jake breathed. 'You're OK. And so are your pups.'

The others had looked back when he stopped and now they joined him.

'Look, the pups are changing colour,' Gabriel pointed out and Jake saw that their coats were no longer grey, but more like their mother's, a lovely rich golden red.

'They're growing up,' Shani whispered.

They watched the little family until the pups grew tired and fell asleep. Then, with the sun dropping behind the mountains, it was time for Jake and the others to continue on their way. But not before another wolf suddenly appeared on a hill nearby and ran down to join Etna at her new den.

'Darkeena,' Gite said softly, and in the next breath, 'Guna too,' as the female that had guarded Etna's pups trotted towards the den.

Jake felt as if his heart was going to explode with happiness and relief. The pack of wolves was gathering at the end of the day to settle down for the night just as others before them had done for centuries. 'It's like they know,' he said, 'that the people are for them again.'

'Yes, it's time we named those pups,' Gabriel agreed.

'I think we should call one Tullu the Second,' Jake said at once. 'To show the world that he lives on through his grandson.'

'Fabulous idea,' said Gite, tears of happiness in her big brown eyes. 'You and Shani can look in the atlas when we get back to find names for the other three.'

With darkness falling, Jake spurred Emperor on behind the others, then pulled him up when a haunting cry pierced the air.

It was a wolf howling, and Jake looked back to see Darkeena standing on the rock next to Etna with his long muzzle lifted up to the heavens. He howled again, a spine-tingling sound that started as a low moan and rose in pitch to become a pure unbroken note.

'You tell them,' said Jake, his hopes rising along with Darkeena's song. 'Tell them that people do care. And that while there are people like Gite and Gabriel and Celia on this earth, there is hope for the Ethiopian Wolves, and every animal in danger.'

This series is dedicated to Virginia McKenna and Bill Travers, founders of the Born Free Foundation, and to George and Joy Adamson, who inspired them and so many others to love and respect wild animals. If you would like to find out more about the work of the Born Free Foundation, please visit their website, www.bornfree.org.uk, or call 01403 240170.